JANE

JANE

When Memories Pause

E L A I N E   B E N S O N

iUniverse, Inc.
Bloomington

JANE
When Memories Pause

This is a work of fiction. All of the characters, names, incidents, organizations, and dialogue in this novel are either the products of the author's imagination or are used fictitiously.

iUniverse books may be ordered through booksellers or by contacting:

iUniverse
1663 Liberty Drive
Bloomington, IN 47403
www.iuniverse.com
1-800-Authors (1-800-288-4677)

Because of the dynamic nature of the Internet, any web addresses or links contained in this book may have changed since publication and may no longer be valid. The views expressed in this work are solely those of the author and do not necessarily reflect the views of the publisher, and the publisher hereby disclaims any responsibility for them.

Any people depicted in stock imagery provided by Thinkstock are models, and such images are being used for illustrative purposes only.
Certain stock imagery © Thinkstock.

ISBN: 978-1-4759-0677-6 (sc)
ISBN: 978-1-4759-0678-3 (ebk)

Printed in the United States of America

iUniverse rev. date: 04/04/2012

ACKNOWLEDGMENTS

I want to especially thank my husband who encouraged me along the way. I am much obliged to my sister, Peggy, who read my book out loud to her husband and gave me the confidence I needed to continue

Several others also deserve credit for seeing me though this project.

I am grateful to Lori Holm for giving me a good review and helpful information.

I would also like to express my thanks to Terry Mejdrich, who if it weren't for him, I would have been at a standstill. He not only helped me through the publishing steps, he also, introduced me to Donna Nelson.

I am indebted to Donna, my sister Karen and nephew Danny for going though my book making corrections and suggestions along the way.

Thanks everyone.

Silhouettes floated around her as if she was in a weightless, empty space. She was one of those shadows. Her body was being absorbed deeper and deeper into a black, sinister abyss. She didn't know why she had allowed her mind to enter that oblivion; or how long she had been there. She was unable to distinguish between what was real or unreal. Time had stopped. Everything was an illusion in an endless void.

Jane started to hear sounds and every once in a while felt as though a switch in her mind was trying to stay on. A light seemed to flicker on for a brief moment, and then all was black again. The sounds would fluctuate back and forth, first high pitched, next low pitched and garbled, making no sense.

"Oh Jane, what's happened to you?" *Ellen's voice was mournful and desperate.*

"Jane, wake up, Jane. It's me Ellen."

The tone of her voice was so familiar, but Jane's mind still wasn't ready to register or accept. "Why can't she remember this person who says she is Ellen? Why is she smothering in this darkness?"

The voice that spoke to her was quiet and soothing. All Jane heard was words that blended together and made no sense. Yet, the calming sound of Ellen's voice brought tears to her eyes.

Jane couldn't stop the dread she felt.

"Oh, please, why do I hurt so? Why don't I want to see?" Jane struggled to keep from remembering. It was to no avail. Thoughts began to flood Jane's once vacant mind. She was just a child and things whirled around in her head so fast it was impossible to focus.

She could feel the cold as it penetrated her body. Jane couldn't seem to think logically. It was as though her mind was unable to cope with reality. The hole she was in was real. It was emitting cold beads of moisture from the earthen wall she was leaning against. The noise was deafening. The horror was unrelenting. Flashes of light and utter darkness were opening and closing in her thoughts. The surroundings were familiar.

"Where am I? Help me."

CHAPTER I

The Massacre

It was the 1700's; the argument of who should rule in this new country had started. The British convinced some of the Iroquois League that what the settlers were planning was wrong. Joseph Brandt, (Thayendanegea), became known as a great military leader of the Iroquois League, and also, because he lived among them, a friend of many colonists. Joseph Brandt was well educated, speaking several languages fluently. Because of Brant's influence among the British as well as the Iriquois League, he was able to persuade some of them to engage in attacks on several towns and settlements in the Mohawk valley.

There was cause for fear and uneasiness amongst the settlers.

———∞◦❂◦∞———

Jenny gently put baby Ellen into the cradle, then moved it closer to the hearth, so as to ensure warmth through the coming night. Her other daughter, Jane, was nine years old. This day would stay vivid in Jane's memory; it was the last time she was to give her mother and father a hug goodnight. Jane heard her mother's soft voice.

"It is time for you to go bed, Jane."

"Can I finish reading this chapter? There are only two more pages;" Jane begged as she sat leaning against the stone hearth of the fireplace.

"You can finish it in bed," said the soft voice again.

"But it's so cozy here, and besides it's too dark in bed."

"Jane!" The voice wasn't so soft now.

Jane reluctantly laid the book on the floor, got up and slowly walked over to her mom who sat in the rocker knitting, bent and gave her a hug and kiss. Then Jane went to the table where her father was reading, and did the same. Finally she went to the ladder that led to the cramped loft above. At the top she leaned down for her mother to hand up the lantern and book. Jane sat the lantern by the corn husk mat she slept on. She put on a warm flannel nightgown, one her mother had made her for Christmas. She crawled under a soft wool lined quilt, another of her mother's creations, snugged into the pillow, and continued to read where she had left off. The crackling of the fire and the soft drones of her parents visiting soon lulled her off to sleep. She never made it to the next chapter.

Jane had no idea how long she had slept when she was awakened by deafening, almost inhuman sounds. It was bright outside, not because the sun was up, but because someone's house was burning.

"Jane!" Jane's father's voice was strange, raspy and frantic as he called her to come down. Her mind was muddled and half alert as she made her way to the edge of the loft. Finding the ladder, she gripped the rung of the first step, then the next, her body trembling from not knowing what was happening outside her once safe home.

Her mother was waiting at the bottom of the ladder. She pushed baby Ellen into her arms; pulled Jane close to her, and held on to them as though to never let them go, pleading, "You take care of her, Jane."

Her father, after he grabbed a rope from a peg by the door, hastened her ahead of him outside and to the back of the house. About fifty feet into a clump of overgrown brush, there was an old dry well. He then tied the rope around Jane, making a hoop to go under her bottom like a swing, then reached and pulled Jane and baby Ellen toward him. Jane could feel the wetness from his tears. A heaving sob wracked his body. He released his grip and lowered them into the well. Jane heard his voice for the last time.

"I love you, Jane! Goodbye!"

Jane clung desperately to the baby, afraid of dropping her into the opening below. The smell was musty. Masses of spider webs stuck to her face, making her want to scream, to reach up to wipe them away, but the words, "you take care of her, Jane" echoed in her ears, causing Jane to hang on even tighter to the baby.

Jane struggled to her feet immediately after hitting the hard ground. Even though it was a dry well, the ground was wet; she felt the moisture as it penetrated her gown the instant she landed. Jane stood up and tried to see her surroundings. She looked up and saw flitting flashes of light as they bounced off the sides of the well. She could see white-hair like strings moving wildly with the stale musty air that filtered through. Jane remembered the thick mass of spider webs she felt on her way down. She shivered at the thought.

Baby Ellen squirmed in her arms. Once again she heard the echoing of her mother's last words to her: "You take care of her, Jane."

Jane prayed the baby wouldn't wake up. As she stood there holding Ellen she began to feel a suffocating tightness in her chest. She hugged baby Ellen a little closer. This brought some comfort; however, the dampness of her hiding place and the unseen terror of what were happening above chilled Jane to the very core her soul.

The horrific noises coming from above kept Jane's mind off the cold. The noises went on endlessly. The Indians were screaming and the victims were screaming even more, only the victim's screams were from pain, agony and suffering. Jane wondered where her parent's were and if some of the screams of pain were theirs. She shuddered and felt an overwhelming tremor of pain shoot through her body twisting into her heart. Jane knew at that moment she would never see her folks again and might die right there in that pit with baby Ellen clutched tightly in her arms. She unconsciously kept her hand over the baby's ear and kept the other ear pressed against her chest the whole time, hoping not to wake the baby. It worked because she slept through the worst. Ellen would never have nightmares from that horrifying incident.

As quickly as the deafening sounds had awakened Jane from her sleep, they stopped. For the moment she could hear the low drones of suffering, her senses were at there highest. She was aware of a nightmare above. The smell of burnt flesh and wood mixed together and the mournful moans as someone took their last breath, terrified her. The popping of a cinder, the smell of blood after the kill, and the eeriness and sense of doom hovered over her like a thick, choking, black fog. Jane wished for the night before. She wanted life to stop then, not in that pit.

Baby Ellen started to whimper. Jane rocked her to and fro, singing "rock-a-baby, rock, rock-a-baby, rock." This worked for only a short time. Ellen was hungry; she had nothing to give her. As the hours went by Jane become more and more fatigued. Baby Ellen wouldn't quit crying. Jane's legs couldn't hold her up; she lowered herself down to the damp ground, pulled her legs up, and wrapped her arms around her knees so she could make a cradle for Ellen. Jane had run out of strength and the will to survive. Her mind went back to the warmth of the fireplace and she imagined herself cuddled beneath her quilt. Jane's eyes focused on the flickering lights above and watched as the last shimmer of light faded and left her in a pit of darkness.

Jane suddenly felt the warmth of someones arms around her. She could hear murmurring in her ear.

"It will be ok, Jane, I am here and I will take care of you."

Jane knew that she was awakening from a dream. She wondered . . . . was it real or a figment of her imagination? Even though the memory was terrifing she felt she could see a glimmer of light trying to penetrate the darkness.

CHAPTER II

Ellen

Ellen arrived at home just as the sun had reached its peak. She came from Albany where she had been attending a boarding school for girls since the first of September, a decision Hugh and Elizabeth made after a lot of persuasion from their daughter. Even though Ellen wasn't quite fifteen, she insisted that she was ready to venture away from the comforts of home, and was excited about going to the city to get her education. She had planned, in a couple of years, to go back to Scotland and finish her schooling. If she moved into Albany now it would be a step toward making it easier for her to adjust to being so far away from her folks later.

Ellen looked older than her age. She had matured a lot the last year; being away from home helped with this. It was very hard for her mother and father to give in to her. She was their baby and she knew they would have liked to have kept her home with them forever. However, seeing the results of what school had done for her made it clear that their decision to let her go was the right one.

Ellen's hair was dark brown, straight, and reached the middle of her back. When running or in the wind, it would billow out behind her and land gently over her shoulders like a soft brown cape. Her eyes were also brown with a hint of green, and when she smiled, they would soften and emit innocence.

Ellen couldn't believe that her sister, who was always the strong one in the family, was lying so motionless and unresponsive. She lamented over how thin Jane had become. The dark circles around her eyes made them look vacant. Her eyes receded into her skull making Jane look even further from reality. Ellen began to hum, 'rock a baby, rock a baby, rock' Ellen felt Jane's body immediately relax, and just as quickly there was an agonizing moan of dread, first just barely audible then louder and louder. Jane's body began to shiver uncontrollably. It took all Ellen had to try to hold her still.

As she comforted Jane, Ellen tried to make sense of it all. She knew Jane lived with terror in her dreams, and Ellen felt she was trying to come back to reality. She would writhe back and forth and guttural noises came from her.

"Help me! I can't get out." Jane's mind screamed, but no noise escaped her lips.

Ellen held Jane closer and murmured, "It will be ok, Jane. I'm here now and I'll take care of you."

After Jane had fallen asleep Ellen questioned Hugh and Elizabeth about what had happened.

"Why is Jane like this, Mother?" Elizabeth said in a broken voice.

"Jane wanted us to come to Duanesburg and get her because she was having difficulty getting over the death of one of her pupils. When we got there she was sitting in her rocker staring into space. It's been difficult to get her to eat and she hasn't eaten enough to sustain her. She is fading so fast, Ellen. It's been three months since we brought her home and she's getting worse. Maybe she can't come back. I think she has given up."

Hugh came in the door and put his arm around Elizabeth's shoulders to comfort her. Ellen could see he was worried that his wife was overdoing it. Elizabeth was becoming depressed and had lost considerable weight.

"I think Jane needs to go into the asylum in Albany, Ellen. Elizabeth wants to see if you can do anything for her first. William Lacy interns at one of the asylums there and said the insane are treated like animals. In fact, William has started giving lectures on a more humane way to treat people who are unable to care for themselves. It would be a last resort before we have Jane committed. I don't think Elizabeth can handle the physical and mental stress of taking care of her much longer. It seems no matter what we do, Jane's health keeps declining and it is getting harder and harder to care for her."

Ellen heard the obvious concern in Hugh's voice. She shuddered at the thought of Jane being put into one of those places. Then, Ellen mustered a boost of energy and began to formulate a plan. If they were unable to bring Jane back, Ellen was determined that she would be the one who would take care of her.

Ellen went into Jane's room and got the rocker and moved it outside. Then she had Hugh carry Jane outside and put her into the chair. Jane was so weak she couldn't hold her head up. Ellen got a small pillow and positioned it to hold her head in place.

"Jane wake up and enjoy the beautiful day."

Jane could hear, and wanted to open her eyes. She just couldn't seem to do anything. "Why can't I wake from this never-ending dream?"

The void turned into realistic and vivid imageries. Jane couldn't seem to make any sense of them. At least her mind seemed to come alive as she slept.

Jane was taken deep into her subconscious mind. She was trying to sort out what was real from the nightmares, the horrors that would sneak into her sleeping state. She seemed to be allowing more memories to come. She really needed to remember those who have cared for her.

CHAPTER III

Hugh Kraufman

Hugh Kraufman, heard the devastating news of several communities being attacked, and rode out to his closest neighbor then the next and the next until he had managed to gather enough men to ride to their aide.

There was smoke rising from several places in the area. The men had ridden for the central part of the Mohawk valley, unprepared for what lay ahead. Cabins were burned to nothing. Bodies were maimed and broken. The smell, retching. Nobody was left alive. They spent a good part of the day burying the corpses. Darkness came upon them and they were forced to quit and make camp for the night.

They picked a spot to camp on the edge of a small Dutch community. Hugh had several very close friends in that village and was afraid of what he would find next. He knew people in the other villages also but only as acquaintances. The people here however, were close.

They smelled the devastation everywhere. It was something that couldn't be avoided, because destruction was everywhere. They made camp and prayed morning would come quickly.

It was too risky to build a fire, so they settled for cold biscuits and venison jerky their wives had packed for them. At the time they didn't think they would need it; however, they were glad they had it then, for they were getting cold and weak. That was the only reason they forced the food down, because none of them felt like eating.

Hugh could understand why, because every bite he took was like eating gravel. He reclined back and stretched out on his blanket. It seemed the more he swallowed, the harder it was to keep his food down. Every once in a while he would take a sip from his flask. He was glad he thought to grab it before he left.

Several of the men had no sooner swallowed down the food, when they were suddenly on their feet and running out of camp. It was impossible for them to keep the food down.

One man was a close friend of Hugh and his family. Hugh weakly got to his feet and went over to comfort him.

"Are you going to be alright, Ben?" Hugh handed Ben his flask of Gin and he took a long swallow.

"I can't understand what is happening out there, Hugh? The family of six that we buried last was my wife's brother and his family. The baby couldn't be more than a couple of months old. My wife helped his wife with the delivery. How am I going to break this news to her?"

"If there is anything Elizabeth and I can do we are willing to help." Hugh couldn't think of any other way to console him. He put his hand on Ben's shoulder and felt a sudden shiver of anguish go through his friend's body.

"How can things go so wrong when there was such joy in that family?"

Hugh sat with his friend until he seemed more relaxed, then helped him to his feet and walked him back to the camp. He handed him the flask one more time and gently guided him to the ground. Hugh then covered him with a wool blanket that he found tied on his friend's saddle.

It was well into the night before they relaxed enough to finally drop off to sleep from exhaustion. Their sleep was fitful and they were jolted awake from the vivid sights and smells left in their minds from the horrendous day. Hugh kept hearing a distant baby crying and couldn't seem to get it out of his head. He rolled over for the third time becoming fully conscious and realized it really was a baby's muffled cry. It seemed a long way off. He yelled for the others to wake up.

"I keep hearing the sound of a baby crying," Hugh said as he revived his comrades. He knew what they were thinking and for all he knew they were probably right.

"Are you sure it wasn't a nightmare, Hugh?" Several dozen voices echoed in the night air.

"It could very well be, however, if there is the slightest chance of someone being alive, we need to find them."

Dreary and half awake the men headed, as quietly as they could, in the direction of the noise. It was coming from the Dutch community. They hadn't gone but a few feet from the camp when they realized the sound was just ahead of them. There was a section that had grown up into a small thicket, which was where it seemed to come from. With lanterns in hand, they carefully made their way into the thicket. Hugh held up his hand and halted the others. There ahead of them was what appeared to be an old well. If they had gone any farther, someone would have fallen into it. The noise was coming from the opening. Hugh got there first.

"My God, there's a baby down there." Hugh was noticably shaken from the realization that what he thought to have been a dream was actually true.

The other men were as touched by the thought of someone being left alive as Hugh was, because there was no sign of life where they had been that day.

Jane was jerked awake from the sound of loud yet familiar voices above. At first, she felt sheer terror and tried to hush the baby. Then a voice from above said gently, "Don't worry, little one. We're here for you."

Jane sensed the instant caring in a familiar voice. She tried to utter a sound, but her throat was too dry. She tried again. A small, urgent, scratchy sound came out; "help."

Nobody had noticed. One of the men had a rope and tied it around Hugh's waist and proceeded to lower him into the well. Dirt and grime sprinkled down onto Jane and the baby, but she didn't care. She and Ellen were about to be rescued.

Hugh could not believe what his eyes were telling him; there was a small child of no more than nine or ten years old, hunched down on the wet ground; a small bundle in her lap. Hugh spoke as gently as he could so as not to frighten the child.

"Hi, my name is Hugh. I'm here to help you".

"Hi," the voice as before.

"It's ok, little one. You don't need to speak"

Hugh reached down, took the baby and handed her up to waiting hands above. Then he picked up Jane. She was small for her age and Hugh had no problem as he lifted her up to another set of hands. The men then helped as Hugh pulled himself out of the well.

Hugh removed his jacket and draped it over the girls, hoping to put some warmth back into their small bodies. Then he got onto his horse and one of the settlers lifted Jane up to him. He positioned her in front, and then was given the baby to cradle in her sister's arms for the journey ahead.

Hugh hated to leave the men. He knew what was ahead for them. However, all he could think of now was getting those children and his own, to a safe place.

Before leaving, Hugh got the attention of his friends and neighbors. "If you feel it nessessary, go home to your families. Right now they are of more importance. If you have family in Albany I suggest you take them there. They are no longer safe in the wilderness."

It wasn't until daylight that he realized that the girls belonged to his friends, James and Jenny Cochren.

Hugh remembered the day he met James. They were on board ship headed for the New World, a land of promise and wealth. Now their bodies would be buried on this land.

Hugh Kraufman was a new comer in the New World and never realized there was so much unrest among the settlers and the Natives. He and his wife, Elizabeth, with their two boys, Hugh Jr. age 14 and Daniel age 12, bought a cabin from a farmer who had given up the wilds of the wilderness and moved into Albany. Hugh was beginning to understand why.

Hugh was a hard working well-built individual. He had been a mason in the old country, and therefore had acquired a sturdy build. He didn't need to wear a hat for his thick, red; shoulder-length hair was enough to keep out the cold. He was dressed in buckskin pants and a long-sleeved wool shirt with a buckskin jacket over the top. He was glad to have had the jacket with which to cover the children.

Except for an occasional whimper from the baby, they were silent throughout most of the trip. Hugh was thankful the baby slept, because they had little to feed her. A few hours into the trip back home, Hugh stopped and heated up some cornmeal mush that was left over from breakfast. He watched Jane do as she had done that morning put some of the mush on her finger and let the baby suck it off. This seemed to have satisfied the baby so far. The trip was slow because Hugh didn't want to chance the children falling off the horse, so he kept the horse at a walk most of the way. Also, he wanted to stay off the main road for fear the enemy would come back and spot them. The going was a lot ruffer when going through under brush, yet, it was safer.

Hugh brought Ellen and Jane to his log home. It was getting late in the day by the time they reached their destination. He wearily dismounted his horse and helped Jane and the baby down. Jane staggered, and then regained her footing with the aid of Hugh's strong hands that balanced her.

As Hugh stepped through the cabin door a lady turned startled. Their eyes met. She could see the concern and anguish in his eyes and knew instantly there was more that she didn't see.

CHAPTER IV

Elizabeth

Elizabeth's husband had a bundle in his arms. She heard a small whimper. She took another step toward him and he handed her the bundle. Her heart paused, while, warmth of love swept in.

Next, she spotted a dirty faced, bedraggled child that was standing behind her husband. The child's eyes were filled with grief and empty thoughts. They were deep blue, and in the night shadows, looked black, darting flashes of fear. The flannel gown she had on was wet and muddy. The bare feet that stuck out from beneath were the same. She wore Hugh's heavy leather coat draped over her shoulders and her small frame struggled to stay standing. Elizabeth handed the baby back to Hugh, and then held her hands out to the girl. Jane was hesitant as Elizabeth drew her small body into the sanctuary of her arms. Then, Elizabeth led Jane into her bedroom so she could change out of her wet clothing and clean up.

After Hugh laid the baby on the bed; he got out the round wooden tub, used for washing clothes, and handed it to Elizabeth. Elizabeth took the tub into the room where Jane was. Then she went to the fireplace and got a pot of water that was always kept full so there was hot water available when needed. As Elizabeth was doing this, Hugh went outside to the well for a bucket of cold water to add to it.

Elizabeth entered the bedroom and found Jane sitting on the edge of the bed shivering, whether from the cold or fear, she knew not what. Elizabeth took her in her arms and held her until the shivers subsided. She then gave her a dry gown.

"When you're through bathing you can put on this nightgown and lie down by the baby to rest." Elizabeth instructed.

She left Jane to bathe and went into the other room to discuss with her husband what they were to do next. After explaining the horrific events of the day, he gave instructions to Elizabeth.

"Elizabeth, we need to pack what is necessary and go to Albany as quickly as we can. Things aren't good in the valley right now. You can't imagine the devastation going on out there. I think the unrest in the valley, just erupted."

"I'll prepare to leave as soon as I feed the baby." They could hear the baby fussing and crying in the next room.

As she spoke, Elizabeth was preparing some warm milk for Ellen. Then she got the baby and brought her out to the front room so she wouldn't bother Jane. As soon as the baby was fed and comfortably asleep, Elizabeth put her on the bed, where Jane was curled up, and already sleeping.

Elizabeth then gathered what they would need for the days that lay ahead. She packed light to make the trip faster and easier on the team. Hugh hitched up the wagon and brought it around to the front of the cabin to load. He called the boys down from the loft so they could help with some of the loading. Then Hugh carried the girls' first one and then the other and set them gently into the wagon, trying not to waken them. Jane was agitated for a time; however, extreme fatigue caused her to collapse back into her dreams. Hugh wondered if they were good ones or dreams of horror. They then began the journey to Albany. His family would stay with Hugh's brother until the fear of attack had passed.

All this was a blur in Jane's mind as they left on the fifty mile trek through treacherous territory, heading for the safety of Fort Albany.

Jane was awakened to the rumble of the wagon as it hit ruts in the trail. They were taking a pathway through the woods. It was a route Hugh had discovered the last time he went to Albany for supplies. He thought it would be the safest way for them; the settlements on the main roads seemed to be the targets of the enemy.

Jane was disorientated and fear swept though her as she started to remember the horror of what had happened. She listened as Hugh and Elisabeth talked lowly to each other. It reminded her of the night before and how comforting it was to hear the low drone of her folks' voices and how safe she had felt.

Jane didn't want to know what was happening. She already knew it was horrific. She started to weep silently and then the sobs became uncontrollable. Elizabeth turned around and took Jane into her arms and held her. Elizabeth didn't say anything, just held her. What could she say to her? That she was safe now? Elizabeth knew that Jane could sense the fear in her.

Elizabeth held Jane until daylight. It was a long tiring night for them. Hugh was up all night. The two boys, however, were able to doze off. They had stopped long enough so that Hugh Jr., the older son, could change places with his father. At which time, Elizabeth gave each of the children a biscuit that she had made the day before and passed around a cup of water that they all drank from. There was only a dozen or so biscuits left to sustain them until they reached Fort Albany.

They made it to the fort in a record two and a half days. They were very hungry and tired and didn't know whether they wanted to eat first or just go straight to bed. However, Hugh's brother's wife, Helen, insisted they sit down and partake of some chicken soup and bread before they retired. Everyone had eaten hungrily, talking very little. Their hunger satisfied, they went right to bed and slept soundly for the first time in two days.

Now that they were inside the safety of the fort, and comfortably settled into Robert's home, things started to feel more normal again. Hugh took a day to rest, and then decided that he needed to return to the valley. After making sure his brother was up to taking in such a large family, and Robert assured him it was ok, Hugh was gone.

Robert had obtained property in the city right after Hugh and he had come to Albany. He had built a home of brick like the Kraufman home back in Scotland. It was a large home with several bedrooms on the second floor and several more on the main floor. In other words, there was room enough that they could all live in comfort. Robert had given them the upstairs. There was a room for the boys to share, one for Elizabeth, and one for Jane and the baby.

Robert and his wife, Helen, was a beautiful couple. Robert had hair the same color as Hugh's, and his wife's hair was a contrasting black that flowed down to the middle of her back. Their personality was as beautiful as they were. Jane became instant friends with their daughters Emily and Helen.

Emily was ten, the same as Jane, and had an inventive mind. She kept Jane busy and therefore kept her mind off the fate of her parents. Emily was hilarious, and would make Jane laugh at her mischievous antics. Helen, on the other hand, was quiet and liked to sit and read. Of course, reading was also something Jane liked, so she hit it off with Helen as well.

As time went by and with the care Jane and her sister received from Elizabeth, as well as everyone else, Jane found she was adjusting to the new life and the pain was easing. That was when she was busy, because it seemed that every time she was alone, the sounds and smells would flood back into her mind. The thoughts brought memories and pictures of her parents. Jane would see them being mutilated and burned. If she was awake and had these thoughts she would run and run to rid her mind of them. If she were asleep, she would wake up screaming and Elizabeth would come to her and hold her in her arms. Jane got so she welcomed the security she felt when Elizabeth was with her. They became very close those first weeks they were together in Albany.

It was during that time that Elizabeth came to Jane and asked her if she wanted to live with them permanently.

"Will you take baby Ellen, too?" Jane asked as she clutched Ellen to her.

"Of course she'll come with us, Jane."

Elizabeth was peeling potatoes for supper as she tried convincing Jane everything would be okay.

Do to complications during the birth of her last child, Elizabeth thought she would never have a daughter, and here she was with the possibility of two. They hadn't been able to locate any of Jane's and Ellen's family.

"Are you sure you don't have any family around here, Jane?

"There is no one that I know of."

Jane flinched as her thoughts flashed back to another time. It was a month before her seventh birthday. One that she would celebrate on board ship bound for America. She could feel and see those last days as though it were yesterday instead of three years ago.

It was a cold and far away place. She could see her mom and her real father. It was bitter and uninviting. Jane recalled never being happy there except when alone with her mother. She never told the Kraufman's about her father in Holland. In fact, she had never told anyone this secret, because her fear of him made it easier to hide his existence.

Jane had never talked to anyone about her life prior to James and her mother Jenny. She didn't see any reason why she should mention it to Hugh and Elizabeth; as long as they didn't know that Jane had a father in Holland anyway, it seemed so unnecessary for Jane to bring it up. Some memories were meant to be kept hidden. Jane considered James her real father and now it was Hugh and Elizebeth she would hold dear. These people were the ones she wanted to remember. However, memories that were buried deep into her mind were coming foreword. So vivid, she felt it were yesterday. Jane was back in Holland living in a mansion.

Jane's real father, Casper, was a large man. His hair was thick and dark brown. It had a natural curl to it and even though he let it grow it was only shoulder length. He would be very handsome if he didn't always have a scowl on his face. Jane felt him to be an unhappy man. She had longed for him to take her into his arms and tell her he loved her.

When Jane's father was home he had her studying. She was only six and all she remembered was studying when she was with him. She loved to read and was a fast learner. She thought maybe that was because it was the only time Casper showed her any admiration and Jane was starved for some kind of affectation from him. Jane felt her father was unhappy with her being a girl. That was why Jane's alone time with her mother were her most treasured memories.

Jane would go up into the room where her mother spent so much of her time sewing, and sit at her feet while she worked.

Jane thought of her mother, Jenny, and could see her, in her minds eye, as though she were in the next room. She had auburn hair that she let flow over her shoulders and down her back. Her hair was long enough that she could sit on it. She always wore her hair up when she was out of the turret room. However, Jenny liked to wear it down when it was just the two of them at home. Jenny had deep blue eyes similar to Jane's. Her dark eyebrows outlined them and made them look sad and disheartning. However, when Jane looked into them they would glow love, and adoration back at her. They were always happy when it was just the two of them.

CHAPTER V

Jenny

The mansion was hidden in a valley nestled deep in the mountains that divide Luxemburg from Holland. The mansion and the grounds all seemed immense in the eyes of a child. There were trees on the hills that surrounded the edge of the valley. The valley was lush green in the summer and white with snow in the winter. There were barns for Casper's work horses, and barns for the other animals. About a mile past the barns there was a cluster of small thatched roof cabins that the workers lived in. If it weren't for the way Casper treated them they would have loved it there.

Casper Cochern was rich, made richer in the making and selling of Gin. It seemed the richer he got the angrier he got. The angrier he got, the more withdrawn Jenny became.

The main reason for Jenny's unhappiness was because of how estranged Casper had become. Casper never ventured much farther than his office while in the country. The only time Casper had any connection to Jenny at all was when he was ranting and raving, and it had become more than Jenny could tolerate.

Jenny was a very different person after she left Casper and came to the New World. While at Rock Haven, the name given to Caspers property, Jenny was frail and hardly ever left the tower room. It got so Casper spent more time at his house in Amsterdam than with his wife and daughter. As the years passed he became more and more alienated from them.

Jenny had never minded him being away all the time because it was while he was gone that she and Jane were their happiest.

When Jane was very young they spent a lot of time outside. They would walk the grounds and take in all the sights of the seasons; from romping in the snow in the winter to picking wild floweres in the summer. Jane would laugh bringing a smile to Jenny's lips as they played games of hide and seek. Jane running as her mother chased after her. Then Jenny began to spend all her time in the tower. It had been a while since she had spent time outside with her daughter. Jenny's mind seemed far away; she had a blank look in her eyes so much of the time.

It was the day Casper's brother, James, appeared that brought the sparkle back into Jenny's eyes. The servants and all the other farm workers had gathered to greet the lone rider as he trotted his horse up the long path to the mansion. Jane was outside and saw how the rider looked like Casper except his hair was thick and red and didn't have the natural curl that her father's had.

Jenny heard Jane as she ran up the tower stairs to tell her of the visitor. She was standing at the window hanging on weak from what she saw below. Jane helped her back to her chair.

"Mother, as you see, we have a visitor."

"Yes, we do." Jenny's voice was faint as she became aware of who her visitor was.

Jenny had left the turret room for the first time in months. She had barely enough energy to walk down the stairs to greet the visitor.

Jenny felt faint as her hand touched James' after almost ten years. The static between them was overwhelming. Jenny pulled her hand back. James looked deeply into her eyes.

"How are you, Jenny?" His voiced quivered.

"How do you think I feel?" Jenny's hand went up to strike him. However, she was so weak it was hardly a slap.

"Whoa there, girl," James grabbed her hand. Jenny lost her footing. James steadied her. She felt his strength and longed to give in and fall into his arms. But her anger at that moment was as strong as her desire and she was able to regain her composure.

"It's been years and not a word from you. I am married to Casper, James. I have been married to him for seven years," Jenny exclaimed, her lips trembling.

"I tried to reach you, Jenny. I sent many letters. I know some of them probably never made it but I can't believe that none of them did. I figured you to have forgotten about me and married, so I quit writing."

"How could you think I would ever forget what we had together? Because of the feelings I have for you my marriage to your brother has been a travesty. In fact, I don't think you should be here when he comes home." Jenny felt a sudden chill.

After exchanging words of anger and trying to fiqure out what went wrong, they knew the feelings they had when James left all those year ago, were the same. Jenny thought they had three or four days at most before Casper came home.

James brought vibrancy back into Jenny's life. Her eyes sparkled like they used to. It seemed that Jenny and James were laughing all the time as they caught up on all the news of James' life since he left Holland for the new world.

James told Jenny he had bought land and built a home in the wilderness.

Jenny took a few minutes to remember the sad beginning.

"James and his brothers, Robert and Casper, had gone to New Amsterdam to start a new life. Casper didn't like it and came back to Holland. Much to Casper's disappointment, James and Robert stayed on. Because of Casper's frustration with his brothers and what he felt was their disloyalty to their country, Casper cut off all ties with them."

Jenny wasn't to tell Jane the details of her and James' prior life until later, at which time Jenny told Jane the love story and sad details of how she and James had become separated. Now James was back and Jenny feared for his life and knew that it wouldn't be good if Casper were to come home and find his brother there. James had to leave immediately. Jenny chose to leave with him. They all boarded a ship going to a land very far from Rock Haven and far from Casper. So it was that at the tender age of six Jane was to leave the only place she had ever known.

They moved into the cabin James had built. Jenny and Jane were to make new friends. Three years later Jenny gives birth to a new sister for Jane. The happiness in this family is unsurpassed.

"Mother, what happened between you James and Casper?" Jane was only nine, but Jenny decided it the right time to let her daughter know what had happened.

"James and I met and fell in love the year before the brothers left. James had promised that he would be back for her as soon as he established himself. However, she had never heard from James and before she knew it Casper had convinced her that something had happened to him."

Out of loneliness and the need for companionship, and at Casper's insistence, Jenny began to go places and do things with him. It wasn't long before Casper asked Jenny to be his wife. Jenny held off for two years and when she never received word from James she finally agreed to marry

Casper. The feelings Jenny had for James never left her and she never had those same feelings toward her husband.

The three years Jane spent with her mother and new father, James, were some of the happiest times she remembered. However, throughout the years, since the brutal massacre of her small community, Jane came to be almost as happy and content with the Kaufmans.

Jane wondered why she was remembering this. That was so long ago. Was this when she started to suppress her memories? Jane was not a little girl anymore. She wondered what she had become. She fought to scream. She fought to speak. She fought to wake up to reality. It seemed the dreams were never ending.

Chapter VI

Road to Recovery

Jane stirred in her sleep and dreamed of how Hugh was the one to rescue Ellen and her from the well. It seemed that the memories kept awakening bit by bit. Every night after she fell to sleep Jane was taken on another route. Sometimes those dreams were so terrifying she was jolted awake and left feeling exhausted, and sometime they seemed to soothe her and left her feeling refreshed and ready to take on the future.

Jane's mind faded back into the past as she continued to unravel her life. She was back at Albany. Ellen and her life were about to take another turn.

Elizabeth asked Jane if she would like to live with them permanently. Her heart pinched as she thought of the changes that were taking place. Jane knew it was the best thing for Ellen and her to do. She was already glad to have Elizabeth there when Ellen started to cry. Jane didn't know what she would do, especially late at night, if Elizabeth weren't there.

"When will we be going back to the cabin?" Jane asked, as she walked back and forth, carrying Ellen. She felt uneasy about how quickly everything was happening.

"Not until things are back to normal in the valley." Elizabeth said as she put the potatoes on to boil.

"In fact, Hugh wants to send us back to Scotland until things settle down here. My family wants us to stay with them. Where we will be safe. They have a whole library of books. James, Hugh, and you will have the advantage of proper schooling while we're there."

Jane knew in her heart that this would be the best thing to do. She sighed and took Ellen to the cradle, and gently laid her down. She turned to Elizabeth who was busy preparing dinner and asked if she could take a short walk before it was time to eat.

"That's fine Jane, but don't go too far. I will worry; young ladies should have an escort."

Jane felt the need to run and take in some fresh air. "I'll be ok, Elizabeth."

Jane stepped outside and looked to see what direction she would take. Being in town wasn't the same as in the country. Even though, Robert had a beautiful home and some land to go with it, Jane felt she was too confined. She thought back to the quietude of the secluded little cabin she had lived in for the past few years.

Jane decided to go the opposite direction from town. She took several deep gulps of air before starting out on a dead run. She ran about a half mile, and then decided it was time to turn around. On the way back Jane took her time to ponder her future. She felt an overwhelming sense of worry for her baby sister and herself. It seemed so bleak. She felt there was no better salution than to live with Hugh and Elizabeth. Jane knew they would be well cared for and loved.

Jane entered the house just as everyone was setting down to eat. Elizabeth was having a hard time letting the servants do the work. Hugh gave her the eye and pointed to the chair.

"You better get used to the servants, Elizabeth; because you will have to let them do their job, after you get to Scotland. Your folks will think I made you into an uncivilized human being."

"I know I do, Hugh, but I like to do things for myself."

"You deserve to be taken care of for a while; after all the hardships of the last few years."

Hugh looked lovingly into his wife's eyes. Their gazes held for a few seconds as if a magnetic pull were drawing each other's deepest thoughts from the core of their inner selves. Hugh had just gotten back two days ago and planned to stay until he saw his family on the boat for Scotland.

"I will miss you, Hugh. I wish you would come with us."

"I am needed here. I must defend what we have. This is where our home is. I will be bringing you home as soon as it is safe."

Jane was only ten years old and already knew the loss and loneliness this family felt. This was the first time her heart went out to them. She was suddenly filled with gratitude and caring for this family. They had been together for almost a month and Jane already felt welcome into their fold. Hugh Jr. and James already treated her like a little sister. Jane already had to put them in their place. Hugh Jr. was four years older and Daniel two years older than Jane and thought just because they were boys they could tell her what to do.

The day had come for the departure of his family. Hugh saw Elizabeth and the children on board the ship headed to Scotland. Elizabeth clung to Hugh. He had to gently pry her free. After yells of endearments and waving until Hugh was just a speck in the distance, Elizabeth took them to their cabin. It was a small six by six box with bunks built into the wall. It would be a cramped trip; however, they should be thankful because they were fortunate to have a cabin. Many of the passengers slept on deck. They were lucky because Angus Macdonald, Elizabeth's uncle, was the owner the fleet of ships they were sailing.

Elizabeth told Jane about the home her family had and how life there would be different than what they were used to here. She never would have thought Elizabeth to come from such a wealthy family. She fit so well in the wilderness and seemed to know how to do all the things working people do.

The trip to Scotland was a long and tedious one, without incident. The weather was nice the whole way. Jane felt nervous because she remembered the last time she was on a long journey over the ocean. At that time the weather was stormy almost every day. The boat would heave high upon the waves and come crashing down with such force it left Jane and her mother dizzy and sick. Jenny spent most of the trip in the cabin. She was too sick to leave. As for Jane, her new father, James Cochern, thought she would be washed off deck by a rolling wave.

It was during that first trip to the New World when Elizabeth and Hugh first met James and Jenny, and that was Jane's first encounter with their children, Hugh Jr. and Daniel. They were rowdy and had no fear of the storm. Nothing ever seemed to bother Daniel and Hugh Jr. Everything was an adventure to them. Jane was envious of them because their parents let them go up on deck whenever the weather permitted.

Jane's thoughts switched from on board ship to America and where she first encountered the Kruffmans to being in Scotland and living with them. Though those thoughts were muttled, they continued to come forward.

While in Scotland the war for independence began. Jane got a good education and the access to books was unbelievable. Jane dreamed to teach some day. Even though women could be a governess, it was frowned upon yet for women to teach at schools; however, she was determined she would break that tradition.

Jane had become close to Elizabeth's mother, Margret, and wasn't in Scotland very long before she called her Nana the same as the other grandchildren.

Jane was in her usual spot on the hearth reading in the massive library when she felt someone in the room besides her. She looked up just as Nana voiced "Goodness child, are you already up and reading."

"I couldn't wait to read more poetry by Jonathan Swift. We only have some of his writings back home and I have yet to read them."

Jane became a good reader very young. She could already read fluently by the time she turned six. She also studied French and Latin. And her mother continued teaching her after they came to America. So while at the McDonald's home in Scotland those three years Jane was able to aquire a lot more knowledge.

By the time she was to go back to America she had read most of Shakespear, John Dryden, and Tristram Shandy. The later being one of the newest books written.

"Where ever did you get so many books Nana?"

"Most of these books have been in the family for many years."

"I never realized there to be so many women authors. I have just finished reading '*The Countess of Mongomery's Urania*' by Mary Worth. It is a romance and I don't know if Elizabeth will approve or not."

"Probably not, but I do know that Elizabeth was reading everything in sight when she was your age, she will most likely turn a blinds eye."

"My real mother loved to read also. She read to me many sonnets and poem when I was young. I loved to listen to the sound of her voice, even though; I never really understood all of what they were about."

"That is what put the love of reading and learning in you, Jane."

"I do believe so, Nana, because I can hear my mother's soft voice as I read."

"Your mother must have been a wonderful person, Jane."

"She was. I shall cherish her memory forever. I only wish my sister could have known her like I do."

"You will have to be the one to bring the memory of your mother to her, Jane."

Jane had already found herself singing the songs she remembered her mother singing to her and had every intention of reading the same verses and stories to Ellen.

"I rather doubt I will need the knowledge of all the books I've been reading here in Scotland." Although, Jane had already decided if she were ever to teach she would surely pass on those Authors and stories to her students.

When Nana turned to leave, Jane put her book down and went to give her a hug. "I'll never forget you and what you have done for my sister and me."

"It has been a pleasure having you here Jane. These last three years have been great. I'm afraid that it is going to be way to quiet after you leave."

"Do you think the war is about to end Nana?" Jane couldn't stand to think of giving up the library.

"It sounds as though it's about to subside. However, one can never tell about these things."

"I am sure going to miss this library when I leave." Jane said with a deep sigh.

"Take all the time you need, Jane and while you are at it pick out a couple of books you would like to take with you when you leave."

"Oh, Nana, you are so kind. I am going to miss you dreadfully." Jane impulsively gave Margret another heartfelt hug.

Later they received word that Hugh would be on the next ship to Scotland; the colonies had become independent.

Daniel and Hugh Jr. were the first ones ready and were waiting for Jane, Ellen and Elizabeth, in the carriage. "Will you please hurry mother. We will be late to meet father."

"I'm almost ready. Elizabeth yelled back at her boys." She was tying Ellen's bonnet and then had to take one quick look at herself to make sure she look ok."

Jane noticed this and smiled to herself. She wasn't quite fourteen and yet she understood the importance of looking just right when you were to see your husband for the first time in three years.

"You're beautiful, Elizabeth. Hugh won't be able to resist you."

When they arrived at the port they could see the sails of the ship bobbing in the bay with about a dozen other ships. They could tell the one that had just gotten in because the men and women were being brought to the dock in smaller boats. The portsman, who worked for the McDonald fleet, had spotted the ship about an hour out and had sent someone to get the family. It looked as though they had gotten there just in time to greet Hugh as he stepped on solid ground for the first time in over a month.

"Is that Father?" Daniel was the first to spot Hugh.

"It is." There was a chorus of several voices.

Hugh's thick red hair could be seen from afar. He was very thin and pale. The horrors of war had noticably taken its toll. He was getting his bag from the boat when he heard the voices of his children. He sat his bag on the ground and looked up. Hugh spotted his beautiful family and leaving his bags, ran to greet them.

He grabbed his wife first and hung on as though to never let her go, and until he heard the protests of his children, he didn't.

Daniel clung to his father first. Hugh looked his youngest son up and down. He had grown a good foot taller since he had last seen him. He was fifteen now and almost ready to leave home for boarding school. One thing Hugh and Elizabeth had decided early on was that their children would have a good education. Especially since Hugh had family in Albany with whom they could stay until they would become old enough to go to Scotland and finish their education.

When Hugh reached out to his oldest son and held him close, he was to realize that Hugh Jr. was at that precise age. "Hello, father, it's so good to see you."

"It's good to see you too. My, it looks like I'm going to be looking up at you from now on. You've become a man Hugh Jr."

Hugh flinched when he thought that his oldest may not be coming home with them.

After hugs and a thousand questions, asked in side of a minute, Hugh held up his hand and halted them. "Okay everyone, we will be home in a few minutes and I will take time to answer all your questions."

Hugh was so busy with the rest of the family he didn't notice little Ellen. She was cowering behind Jane. Hugh reached out his hand and she hid further behind her sister. Ellen was only a baby when Hugh left and had never gotten to know him.

However, it didn't take long before she was calling him father.

It had been a week since Hugh had arrived. He was already starting to get his color back. Everyone was satisfied with all the questions they had. It was time to prepare for the journey back to America,

"We need to get our things together. If we wait too much longer we could hit some bad weather." They were at the table eating breakfast and Hugh thought he would tell them his plans while they were all together.

"Are you sure you are ready to travel so soon?" Elizabeth was concerned for her husband's health.

"We really don't have a choice, Elizabeth. I need to get back to the farm and if we don't leave soon we will have to stay the winter. I will not take my family across the ocean when there is danger of bad weather. We are now free from English rule in America and things are finally calm in the valley. It's time to go home." Hugh's voice had the tone of finality.

Chapter VII

The Past Unfolds

Jane woke to a beautiful day. It had been several days and things were becoming clearer and clearer. When Ellen came to her room to help her get ready for the day, Ellen was shocked to see Jane had gotten up on her own.

"Good morning, Jane. Are you sure you're strong enough to be up and about without any help?"

Jane turned toward Ellen and tried to smile and form words. They were spoken so softly that if Ellen hadn't read Jane's lips she wouldn't have been able to understand her. Jane could see the relief in Ellen's face when she looked at her. This was the sign of communication that they were all waiting for.

Ellen went to Jane, beaming, and gave her an almost never-ending embrace. Jane returned the gesture with a weak response. Jane now knew that Ellen was the baby she had held so tightly in the well. The dreams were real.

Ellen walked Jane to the commode and helped her finish dressing. Then they preceded arm and arm into the front room without hollering for help. Jane leaned on Ellen for support. Elizabeth was fixing breakfast and didn't notice right away. They walked up behind her and Jane said in a low gravelly voice.

"Hi, Mother!"

Elizabeth turned around until face to face with Jane. Tears flooded her eyes. She took Jane into her arms and said over and over, "I'm so glad your back; I'm so glad your back."

From that day on the road ahead was easier for Jane. She started talking more and more and regained strength. It was yet another week before she could talk normal and knew Ellen was waiting for Jane to tell her what happened. How could she tell Ellen when she didn't know herself?

Thoughts kept going through Jane's mind. She wondered, but doesn't really want to know, why she was there instead of in Duanesberg teaching. Jane remembered the day she left for Duanesberg. It seemed only yesterday. Yet, Ellen was so grown and going to school in Albany. Jane wondered where that little girl was, the one whose tears she dried before she left.

The memories swirled around in Jane's mind so fast she found herself holding her head as she tried to slow them down. Closing her eyes she tried to put those memories in order.

Jane found herself remembering the day Hugh came to get them in Scotland. She could vaguely remember him getting off the boat. It had been so many years. When Hugh hugged her she remembered how safe she felt in his arms.

Jane had spent ten wonderful years with Hugh and Elizabeth. She had grown to love them as her own parents; even though she could never bring herself to tell them so. It was as though Jane would have to give up her real parent's spot in her heart. Jane wasn't ready for that yet.

Ellen had grown to be a beautiful young girl. She was happy and carefree, and had no pain of what they had lost. She called Elizabeth mother as she had from the first. Hugh and Elizabeth loved her as if she was really theirs. This was the important thing for Jane, because now Jane knew she could leave Ellen behind and begin a new life feeling comforted at knowing Ellen was in loving hands.

It was early August; and the sun was just peaking at the edge of the world. Jane felt as though she was about to lose the security and connection of a place that was dear to her. Yet, the urgency and excitement she felt about the future outweighed this loss. She was about to start a new life.

Jane walked once again up the steep pathway that led to a spot she had visited almost every morning since coming to live with the Kruffman's. However, this morning was different; it would be the last visit she would make for some time. Jane sighed as she brushed her long hair back over her shoulders. Hair that flowed in soft dark waves down to her waist; Jane hadn't taken the time to put it up in a bun, her usual style. Her eyes were a deep blue, they accented her face and if you looked into them too closely, it seemed the memories buried there were on the verge of surfacing. Jane had matured into a tall, strong, beautiful young lady. She was no longer the, tiny, frail, little girl Hugh had rescued from the well.

Jane had on a modern style dress that Elizabeth had given her as a special going away gift. The dress had a fitted top, the neckline low, but not too low, and the waist was fitted with a full skirt that reached the ground. The dress was pink with white ruffles around the neckline. It seemed almost too elegant to travel in, but traveling was what she would be doing.

It seemed the closer she got to the top of the hill, the wounds in her heart would once again surface, and visions of that day long ago began. At the top, she looked off over the clearing and toward the dense green forest that filled the valley below. The sun was a bright yellow with streaks of orange on the horizon. Her head turned as if by a magnet toward the direction of the home she had lost many years before. She felt it would be a while before she saw this sight again. She took in a deep breath of fresh air and absorbed the surroundings. Jane never wanted to forget the feeling of tranquility and safety this place had brought her.

Jane looked down toward the cabin. She saw Hugh had finished harnessing the horses. The horses had offered no trouble when he backed them up to a tripple tree and hitched them to the shaft. Jane watched as Hugh stopped what he was doing and looked back at the log cabin.

Hugh's thoughts took him back to when he first came there and the hard work he put into building their home. The cabin had a lean-too off the back and a quaint porch in the front with a bench on one end and a swing on the other.

Then Hugh's mind wandered back to the old country and the cold rock mansion they had called home, and wondered why he had been so distressed when he was run off his land and forced to flee to another country. The happiness he and his wife had here was no comparison to the land wars and continued battle to keep his title in Scotland.

However, Hugh never realized that he would be leaving the hostility of one country, and landing in the start of a revoulation in another. They had landed at Long Island Sound in June of 1771. There was already turmoil amongst the settlers, British, and the natives. Hugh had befriended almost everyone he met, native or otherwise. Jane's and Ellen's folks, James and Jenny Cochern being the first people he met, and seeing as James was already settled in the new world, Hugh had received a heads up from him during the time they were on board ship. Being James had been there several years earlier, he knew the people and the struggles there were when first starting out on untamed land, he was able to help them settle in and meet some of the neighbors.

The community where James and Jenny Cochren had their home no longer existed, leaving Jane and Ellen the only inhabitants surviving its fate. That was when Ellen and Jane had come to live with them, and where they have lived those many years. Hugh knew it would be hard for Jane to leave Ellen. This place had become home to them.

Hugh was proud of the way he built up this once very tiny one room cabin he had purchased thirteen years before. Right off, he had added a bedroom on one end for him and his wife, Elizabeth. It wasn't until the year Jane and Ellen were added to his family of four that he built a lean to off the back. Daniel slept in the loft.

Hugh spotted Jane as she was coming out of the cabin door struggling with a trunk. Jane saw the look of admiration in Hugh's eyes and her heart skipped a beat as she realized she wouldn't have Hugh to turn to when living so far away. Ellen was behind Jane trying to hold up the other end of the trunk. It was to no avail. Hugh left what he was doing and went to Ellen's aide.

"Hey! Can I give you a hand there little girl?" Then Hugh grabbed Ellen's end of the trunk, leaving Ellen hollering and stomping off into the cabin.

"I can do it, Father! I wanted to help Jane."

"Thanks, Father." Jane looked back into Hugh's eyes with adoration. Ellen wanted to help her so much she was sometimes a pest. Jane was really going to miss her though.

"She's going to be lost without you here, Jane. You two have been inseparable since you lost your parents."

Jane winced at the mention of her parents. She had been thinking a lot about them the last few months. It happened like that, she would go a long time with the horror of that night trapped way back into her subconscious and then all of a sudden they and that night were back. It seemed as though she could reach out and touch them they were so vivid in her mind.

Jane struggled as she lifted her end of the trunk into the wagon.

"Are you ready for the long ride ahead, Jane?" asked Hugh

"I guess so. Just how long will it take us to get to Duanesberg?" Jane asked. She had been to Albany often, but never to Duanesberg.

"It's a good three days northeast of here. Actually it's about the same as going to Albany only the opposite direction," replied Hugh, as he settled down the anxious black percherons.

Hugh was pleased with the two massive steeds he had purchased at the horse auction over at Cherry Valley the week before. The owner was known as a good workhorse trainer. Therefore, Hugh was sure he would have no trouble with them while traveling the next few days.

"It should be a great time, providing the weather is good. I think Ellen and Elizabeth need to get away for a while. They haven't been to Albany since last summer and Ellen misses all the pretty things in the shops. Jake's Country Mercantile isn't quite the same."

Jake's was a run-down, age old, wagon stop, named after the owner, Jake McCloud. He kept a variety of food, always had a pan of bean soup on cooking and there was a livery out back where he would board a weary horse and replace a shoe if need be.

"I think Ellen and Mother are both planning to buy some fancy material for new dresses." Jane said as she shifted the trunk to make room for one more.

"Yah, it's a good thing we'll only be spending a couple of hours in town or I'll have to work to pay for all the things they'll just have to have." Hugh chuckled.

"I wish my living quarters would be finished so you could stay a few days and rest up before you go back." Jane would be staying with a farm family until they finished the room that was being added on off the back of the small school house that was to be her future home.

Jane was ready and welcomed the new position. It was rare for a woman to have such a position and Jane was eager and optimistic, ready to prove that she was capable. She didn't want to be a governess to only a couple of children in the city, a position expected of a woman. Jane wanted a classroom full of happy, energetic, children.

Hugh was one person that knew the capabilities of Jane. He had known Jane's strength and determination for ten years now. She had always proved herself as capable as the boys. And Hugh Jr. and Daniel, though showing a bit of jealousy now and again, had come to look at Jane, with different eyes. Jane would be just fine. She can shoot a gun, cook, plant a garden, can food, and do everything else necessary to live. It seemed only yesterday they were a family of six and together. Now with Jane leaving and the boys at school in Scotland, their family would be decreased to three.

Jane knew how much Hugh missed his sons, and how he must have felt a great loss at the thought of her moving so far away. Jane had become very close to Elizabeth and Hugh throughout the years and knew how much she would miss them. However, this was her dream, being on her own and teaching children.

Jane always loved to read and studied every book she could get her hands on. Elizabeth was educated in Scotland before she and Hugh were married. It took Elizabeth a while to be at home in this new country; not that she didn't like it, but because she missed her family. Therefore, it was easier for Hugh when he decided to send Elizabeth and the children back to her folks during the revolution.

It was while they were abroad that Jane's desire to teach was heightened. She was engulfed in books and the more she read the more she wanted to learn and teach what she had learned. Coming home, after the war, Elizabeth had continued to teach them until Daniel was old enough to go to the city and finish his education. What education Jane had gotten was from both her sets of parents and during her stay in Scotland. Jane never had the opportunity to go to finishing school. Mainly because she felt she needed to be with Ellen for as long as she could.

Hugh still had a hard time thinking of Jane working. He thought she should be married and raise a family. However, Hugh knew Jane was a different breed of woman, one that demanded her freedom and independence. Hugh could see the future of this country being run by women. He knew Jane didn't think this would be such a bad idea.

"Jane, you be sure and come back home if things get hard for you, and don't let anyone bully you. If this happens you let me know right away."

Hugh looked old at that moment; he inhaled a long drawn out gasp of air. He knew the Lacy's were good people, and that they would look out for Jane. The Lacy's were the family where Jane would be staying when she first arrived at Duanesburg.

"Don't worry Father; I'll keep a club by my door." Jane laughed, putting her arm around Hugh trying to reassure him.

Hugh returned the hug, and wanted to keep that hold. Then releasing his grip watched as Jane went back to the cabin for another load.

Upon entering the cabin Jane saw little Ellen setting on the hearth crying.

"What's the matter, Ellen?"

"I don't want you to go, Jane. What will I do when you're gone? I won't have anyone read to me at night before I go to sleep." Jane had always read out load to Ellen at bedtime.

"This is good, she said. Then you can read to yourself. You can improve your reading skills a little, you know."

"Oh Jane, it won't be the same. I need you here. Please don't go," cried Ellen.

Jane pulled Ellen to her and comforted her, by rocking back and forth, and humming 'rock baby a rock,' like she did in that well long ago. Jane could hear her mother. "Take care of her, Jane."

Jane closed her eyes tighter hoping to shut out the promise she had made to her mother.

"I have to go mother. Ellen will be fine without me now," she thought. Then Jane let go of Ellen and looked into her eyes saying, "Just think how spoiled you'll get being the only one left at home for Mother to dote on."

Daniel and Hugh Jr. had been gone for years. Actually, Ellen barely knew them. She was only three the last time she had seen Hugh Jr., because he never came back from Scotland when the rest of the family did, and Daniel started boarding school in Albany the same year they came home. Hugh and Elizabeth went to visit every so often, but Jane and Ellen had stayed behind to tend to the livestock and watch the place.

Ellen's face lit up and she wiped away the tears, and ran out the door as though nothing had ever happened.

Finally, they finished loading and were ready to depart. Jane had two good sized trunks that took up a lot of the room in the wagon. However, the four of them had managed to fit in with all the baggage. Hugh then hollered for the team to go and they were off, heading slowly up the long incline to the tote road going north.

When they reached the top Jane had Hugh stop. She then climbed down from the wagon and walked out to the clearing where she had been that morning and knew she would get a clear view of the cabin. It looked so lonely; the only home she could see for miles around. Jane took a deep breath and made herself a promise to come back for a visit soon; then she turned and got back into the wagon. Hugh urged the horses on. There was silence for several minutes when Ellen suddenly yelled with glee.

"There goes a bunny. See him!"

The bunny was scurrying as fast as his little legs could go. He came to a clump of brush and disappeared inside. By the time the little fellow got into the brush, Ellen was already off the wagon and running in close pursuit. She turned with a wide grin on her face and exclaimed. "I'm so glad he got away. I really wanted him though. Wasn't he the cutest and cuddliest, thing Jane?"

"He sure was, Ellen. Maybe Father will get you one of your own to raise?"

Hugh piped up, "Don't make promises for me, Jane. There are already enough of the little critters running around and playing havic with the garden."

The road that led to the main route was full of holes and ruts from the last rain and the going was a rough one. They wondered what the main route would be like. Unfortunately, it was the same, and they prepared for a brutal ride the next few days and prayed that it wouldn't rain. The trees passed by, and for every familiar tree and shrub that disappeared behind them, new and unfamiliar ones were ahead.

The trip proved to be a pleasant one and they enjoyed themselves by bringing up memories from the past. Everyone seemed to gang up on Jane. Telling about the time she made bread and forgot the yeast; they could hardly bite into the biscuits they were so hard. And the time their cat caught a mouse and brought it to her as a gift. Jane had jumped up on the table and screamed for her life.

Two days later they reached the cut off that took them west toward Duanesberg. Another day and a half and they would be at their destination. Hugh expressed to Elizbeth his excitement of seeing William Lacy.

"It's been years, Elizabeth. I can't believe he has so many kids"

Hugh had gotten to know William Lacy during the revolation. He and William were with the same fleet of ships, which were maneuvered by DeGrasse during the war. They had become good friends. Hugh had met his family after the war, but hadn't seen them for some time. He couldn't wait to meet with them again. Suddenly the wagon hit a rut and jarred Hugh back to the present.

He couldn't believe how good the trip had been so far. They had absolutely no trouble with the horses and there had been no highwaymen to rob or harass them. This was proof of how improved the roadways were becoming. Maybe the 1780's would prove to be a turning point for the New World.

There were three added wagon stops in route that kept groceries and goods on hand so the travelers and settlers wouldn't have to travel so many miles for supplies. A couple of the wagon stops along the way had several families settling there making the start of a new community. It seemed to be growing fast.

"Before you know it there will be cities like Albany and New York clear out here." Hugh thought out loud.

Their thoughts of how much safer it had become were suddenly interrupted by loud screeching and hollering. The percherons suddenly took off on a dead run. Hugh tried to hold them down, but to no avail. The more he tried, the faster they would go. The screeching continued with the thundering of horse hooves in close pursuit. Hugh watched, ready to defend his family, as two Indians rode up along side of the horses. One of the Indians jumped on to the horse's backs, and was able to bring them to a stop. Hugh saw the Indians had smiles on their faces; which didn't make him too happy, until he realized one of them was Dave Adams, another aquaintence from the war. He was just a child at the time, not much older than Hugh's own son.

"What are you trying to do?" demanded Hugh as he is shook Dave's hand.

"I didn't want you getting too lax with keeping in tune to what's going on around you. There has been some robbing and harassing in these parts the last few months," said Dave, as the grin on his face faded to a serious look.

"It's not you, by chance?" said Hugh.

Dave smiled a secretive grin and said, "Wouldn't you like to know."

Ellen was so excited at seeing Dave she could hardly set still in the wagon. It was too much for her. She climbed down from the wagon to run off some of the excitement. Dave got down from his horse to chase after her. He picked her up and twirled her around. Ellen giggled and screeched all the while.

Dave, an Oneida Indian, and good friend of almost all the settlers, had befriended the Kraufman family soon after they settled in the valley. He stopped by their cabin a couple of times a month, and spent the day helping Hugh with what ever he happened to be doing, in exchange for a good home cooked meal.

Dave loved to be around the kids and was good friends with Hugh Jr. He and Hugh Jr. were close to the same age. Dave had taught him and Daniel the secrets of hunting, tracking, trapping, and other survival techniques the Indians knew. Later he had taught Jane and was now showing Ellen. Only Dave hadn't been to see them for almost a year.

"What have you been up to, Dave?" asked Hugh.

"We've been scouting land in the west. Our families are settled there now. Hopefully, the new government has enough land so we can rest in peace for a while," Dave said, half joking.

"I hope so, too," said Hugh, as he got down from the wagon and turned to help his wife and Jane down.

"Is it good land for planting?"

"There is some great and some not so great. It's all beautiful, though. Land and earth are always beautiful. There is a great river that runs through the middle and the fish are plentiful."

"What river might that be?" asked Hugh

"It's called the Ohio river," said Dave

"I hear the soil in that area is good for growing corn."

"Yes, and it's looking like a good year. If only we didn't have the nagging fear of our fields being burned. I know it's been several years since the army burned and destroyed our families' homes and crops, but it still haunts my people. They are always looking over their shoulders. I fear my people may still have more trouble ahead with the new government." Dave looked sad as he thought of what was happening to his people.

Hugh and his family felt badly for Dave. They knew what trouble the Indians had with the Europeans and they wished only the best for him. Dave was only fifteen years old when he began scouting during the war. He had helped the settlers and now they turned on him. It didn't seem right.

After Hugh built a small fire, he found a comfortable spot to sit and motioned his friends to sit down to visit while Elizabeth and Jane fixed some lunch. It was an early lunch, but it had been a long time since breakfast and they were all starved. Elizabeth had made biscuits to bring on the trip and fried up some potatoes with onions to go with them. After adding some smoked turkey, it was a feast fit for a king.

Once they finished eating, they sat back on the hillside and reminisced about old times. Dave and his friend Josh were happy to have conversation with someone other than each other. They had been traveling for the past week. They would take different routes each trip in hopes of finding easier and better ways for travel. Many times they had helped the settlers find closer and safer ways to different destinations. Dave was on his way to Duanesberg, also. He had met a young lady there several months earlier and felt he needed to see her again. Ellen was excited about the possible love story. She teased him and wanted to hear more.

"What is her name, Dave?" asked Ellen.

"You don't know her, but her name is Jessica Jones. Her father is the local parson;" Dave said looking over at Jane. "Jessica will be happy to meet someone close to her age."

"Is she nice?" asked Ellen.

"She's not only nice, she's beautiful and I think the feelings I have for her are the same as she has for me," Dave stated proudly grinning even bigger causing his eyes to sparkle.

Elizabeth finally stepped in and told Ellen not to be such a pest. "We'll be meeting Jessica and can check her out ourselves to see if we approve of her for Dave."

"Oh, I'm sure everyone will welcome her. I only hope the townspeople will accept her being my wife. There is a parcel of land about sixty miles north-west of Duanesberg that I hope to buy and farm. I know Jessica will not approve of living in the Indian village. I just hope I will be able to purchase the land," said Dave as he rose to his feet and stretched.

They all followed his motions and prepared themselves for the rest of the ride to Duanesberg. Dave and his friend Josh escorted them the rest of the way.

Jane smiled to herself seeing the obvious devotion and love Dave had found, and she only hoped to find the same some day. She prayed Dave's wishes would be fulfilled. Europeons frowned on inter-marrying with the Indians.

Jane was still daydreaming about love when they spotted a small frame structure with a partially finished room on the back. She knew instantly that it was her new home. They stopped at the school and looked around. It was small; however, it would be fine. The spot where the school stood was in a small clearing that didn't cover more than an acre. This seemed to be a perfect spot with plenty of room for the children to run and play. The only drawback was the cemetery being only a few yards away. Thank goodness there was a narrow stretch of a sparsely wooded area between the cemetery and the school. This made Jane feel a bit more comfortable. She wasn't superstitious or anything, but didn't like the idea of living so close to a burial ground. She hoped she would get used to it.

Hugh unloaded two big trunks, this way Jane would only have to worry about one bag with the necessities that she would need during her stay at the Lacy's. It shouldn't be too long before the room was finished.

Then they were on their way to see the town of Duanesberg and to meet some of its citizens. The Methodist church was only three-quarters of a mile from the school. This was comforting to Jane. Reverend Bogert heard them as Hugh guided the team up alongside the church, and hurried out the door to greet them.

"Welcome to our town," He said with a strong and no-nonsense voice.

"Hello, Reverend, Hugh returned, and then proceeded to introduce his family and friends. This is my daughter, Jane. She is the new teacher."

Reverend Bogert obviously flinched; it probably troubled him to think of a woman teaching the children. Even though, it was happening more and more.

"I hope to see you in church," said the reverend, as he held out his hand in greeting and vigorously shook Jane's.

"I'll be there." However, Jane was unsure whether she liked him or not.

After visiting with Reverend Bogert for a few minutes, and being filled in on the times to be in church, they were off again.

Duanesberg, better known as Brahman's Corner, was a small development in the Mohawk valley. The community was spread out over a large area. The land was made up of rolling hills thickly wooded with a variety of different trees. After the war, communities had started to sprout up all over the valley; Duanesberg, (Brahman's Corner), originally made up of scattered farms, had developed into a thriving town.

Although many of the families had lived here before the war, many more were settling into the small village, bringing with them everything from several churches, a livery, a pub and other stores. There was also a school and a hired teacher. This would be the first lady schoolteacher, and the people were hesitant about hiring her. However, the Lacys recommended Jane because Hugh and Elizabeth were good friends of theirs, and the townspeople decided to chance it.

After meeting several people including Jessica, with whom Jane had hit it off immediately, they were ready to spend the remainder of the time shopping before they continued on to the Lacys'. Elizabeth and Ellen were so excited to see such a big variety store. They hadn't been to town for a long time and were eager to shop. After they filled their arms with necessary and not so necessary items, it was time for them to take Jane to her temporary home.

Jane went up to Jessica and told her that she hoped to see a lot of her when she moved into the school. Jessica was totally taken with Dave Adams. They were a beautiful couple and Jane hoped only the best for them.

"Farewell Jessica, goodbye Dave," Hugh hollered as he climbed back into the wagon.

"I shall see you soon," promised Dave to his friend. "I hope to be in your area in a couple of weeks."

"Great, we will be looking for you." This time it was Elizabeth that answered.

"Bring Jessica," yelled Ellen. They were already moving looking forward to the end of the last two miles, the Lacy's.

CHAPTER VIII

The Lacys

The Lacys lived at the top of a hill about two miles southeast of Brahman's Corner. William Lacy had purchased 400 acres of land and he and his sons cleared a small spot the first year, without the aid of team or plow. They planted some crops and cut down a small stand of aspan from which they gathered enough logs for a small cabin and firewood for the winter. Then, after William and his sons finished construction of the cabin, one that was hopfully large enough to house his large family, William and his second son William, Jr. hiked back to Massachusetts.

The following spring they once again traveled over rough trails and through wilds of the wilderness to bring his family back to their new home. Over the years their log dwelling was enlarged to two floors, five bedrooms, with enough room to accommodate his ever increasing family. Because they had the extra room, Jane was able to stay with them until the addition was finished at the school.

The Lacy children were outside and about a mile up the road waiting to get the first sight of their new teacher. The children were a stair step up from the youngest to the oldest. The youngest being baby Polly, then one year old Lemuel, Hanna two, John five, Mehtilda ten, Sally thirteen, Betsey fifteen, William seventeen, and Thomas nineteen.

The three oldest were the least interested and in no hurry to have an extra person crowding them out of a bed. However, they all changed their mind about Jane the moment they met her. She proved to be fun, and they could feel she had a genuine love of children. Jane had felt welcome and liked by the Lacy's right off.

The Lacy's were a warm and loving family, and even though it was awfully loud and there was always some crisis amongst the children; Jane felt she belonged. She had her first test of what it was going to be like teaching a lot of children at once.

Jane was so taken up with the younger children, and their wanting too all talk at once, that she didn't notice the three older ones. It wasn't until that evening at the supper table that she had her first glimpse of Thomas, the oldest son. In fact, they hadn't been introduced so she didn't even know his name yet. She tried to avoid his stare but their eyes seemed to be drawn to each others like a magnet.

Finally Thomas spoke, "Hello, I'm Thomas, you must be the new schoolteacher?"

Jane swallowed her food so quickly she started to choke. She finally composed herself and turned to nod an acknowledgment. "I'm Jane."

"I hope you enjoy your stay here Jane, and I personally welcome you." Thomas replied.

Polly started to cry in the next room and Beth, William's wife, excused herself from the table to tend the baby's needs.

Jane was relieved for this distraction. The other children began asking her questions about where she had received her education. When she told them she had learned a lot while she was in Scotland, the questions became overwhelming. The children knew the story of how their grandparents had come from across the ocean and wanted to hear about Jane's adventure, too. Elizabeth came back and calmed them down.

"Ok, children, I think Jane needs a break form all the questions." Beth could sense how overwhelmed Jane was.

It was suddenly quiet and then a steady clinking of the utinsels as they all began to eat at once. Before long everyone was off doing their own thing leaving Jane to her thoughts and to getting settled in.

Jane climbed the narrow stairway up to the second level and then another set of stairs to the third level, which was an open room the length of the house. It was unfinished but felt and looked comfortable, an abode until she could move to her permanent dwelling. There was a bed with a feather tick mattress. It was made up with flannel sheets and a cozy quilt made from bright colored materials. There were also two feather pillows at the head of the bed and a braided rug on the floor. There was a tiny window at each end of the room which had cute little flour sack curtains on them.

Jane had fallen immediately in love with her temporary housing and already felt as though she belonged. The boys had carried her bag up to her room. She would keep most of it packed, and would unpack only the necessities she needed for the next few weeks. There was a small commode with a drawer, and a cupboard for a chamber pot. Jane doubted she would use the pot so she took it out of the cupboard and unpacked her night gown and pantaloons and put them neatly into the cupboard. She then put her toiletries, comb and vanity items into the drawer. In the process she had broken the beautiful mirror that Elizabeth had given her for her sixteenth birthday. She felt a temporary moment of loss and struggled to keep from crying.

While unpacking, Jane remembered the quick goodbyes to Hugh and Elizabeth. She was surprised when Elizabeth had handed her a package containing another beautiful dress. It was long and flowing with a fitted waist. It had long fluffy sleeves that fit tight around the wrist. The one she had worn the day they left had short sleeves and a low neckline, where as that one had a high collar with a fitted bodice. That dress was a baby blue with contrasting white where as the other was pale rose with a contrasting white. Jane hung the dress over the privacy board and continued to ponderd the last moments she had spent with the ones she loved most in this world.

The Lacys had served Hugh and Elizabeth coffee and sandwiches, during which time they caught up a little on each others lives. They rested as long as they dared to, and then were ready to begin the journey home. There was so much chaos with the welcoming party Jane barely got a chance to say a parting farewell. Ellen had grabed her around the waist and hung on for dear life. Jane had to pull her away. There were tears and words of endearment then Jane watched sadly as they got back into the wagon for their journey home. It was early afternoon and they wanted to get as far as possable before they stopped for the night.

Hugh had promised they would come to visit Jane, if the weather permited, sometime around Easter. That was a whole seven months away. Jane watched as the wagon disappeared into the distance then turned to her temporary home; her heart and mind were still with her family.

Jane couldn't quit thinking of how Hugh and Elizabeth had treated her so well. She always received something special from Elizabeth for her birthday and Christmas.

The previous Christmas Hugh had made, and Elizabeth decorated, a beautiful hope chest for Jane. The chest was made from the most beautiful cedar. Elizabeth had carved Jane's name and a design on it. There wasn't room for it in the wagon so Hugh promised he would bring it when he came at Easter. Jane would be able to use it as a place to put some of her things that there wasn't room for anywhere else.

"Miss Jane!" Jane was startled by the sound of a child's voice and her arm being shaken. "Miss Jane!"

It was ten year old Mahtilda. She was so cute looking up at her. She had long dark braids and a spray of freckles across her nose that glistened when the sun beams bounced off them.

"What is it Mahtilda?"

"Mother would like to know if you want to ride into Brahman's Corner with them. They are going in for supplies."

"Certainly, tell them I'll be right there." Jane didn't really feel like getting back in a wagon again. But, she wanted to price the cost for a new mirror. She would definitly need one once she moved into her own place. For the time being the Lacey's had a small mirror, on the wall over the commode that she could use.

Some of the citizens were outside when they arrived in town. Jane smiled and waved as they passed by. The Lacys seemed to know everyone in town, and would pause a moment to talk to them. Jane felt that she would come to know everyone, too, and smiled to herself. It seemed a nice place to start a new life.

Next, they stopped at the mercantile. Again, Jane couldn't get over how huge the store was in comparison to the trading post that was close to Hugh and Elizabeth's. In fact, it was almost as big as some of the stores in Albany. There were shelves of different things, from material for sewing, to tobacco for the menfolk. There were jars of licorice and hard candy. Jane had a sweet tooth and grabbed a handful of hard candy to take home for the children and of course to appease her sweet tooth as well. Then, she priced the mirror and decided she had enough extra to purchase it. Jane vowed she would guard this one with her life, because she needed all the money she had left to get settled into her own place.

As Jane neared the counter to pay for her purchases she overheard a couple of people discussing Jessica and Dave. They seemed disapproving of the fact that they were seen walking hand in hand.

"Injun and White don't mix."

Jane couldn't help but feel a stab of pain as they were talking about two very lovely people. In fact, they were speaking about two people who were in love. Jane quickly paid for the mirror and left the store before her

45

temper flared. She didn't want to start off on the wrong foot the first day there

After more words of welcome from people they passed, Jane realized there were many who seemed to understand that people are people no matter what. Before long they were on their way back to the farm. It was a pleasant evening, the ride was relaxing, and Jane relished the thought of curling up on her bed and sleeping the night away. She already felt at home with the Lacys and knew she had made permanent friends. As she dreamed of her possible future, Jane felt a wave of contentment and happiness. Her dreams of being a teacher were becoming a reality.

CHAPTER IX

Thomas

Jane's stay at the Lacy's proved to be a good one. She and Thomas had developed a close relationship. It seemed they could talk about anything and Jane felt she had found someone to fill the void in her heart. The only bad thing was Thomas and William would be leaving for Harvard College the following week. Thomas promised to write and keep Jane posted on what he was learning.

Thomas did correspond with her, and Jane received the first letter while she was still at the Lacy's. The younger children teased her, their eyes beaming as they did so. They were as excited about the relationship as Jane was. The letter from Thomas made her heart rush. Jane read it over and over, feeling as though she was on a cloud and that life was about to reach a new era. She picked up the letter and read it again.

Dear Jane,

Thanks so much for your letters. Receiving them will make the days go by faster. You ask how I like college. Well, there's nothing like learning about agriculture, but hands on is what I like best. When we are out in the field it's great, but being penned up in a room is not my cup of tea.

My dream is to have a farm of my own, which I'm saving every spare dime for. I have a part-time job keeping books for a store here in town, and don't spend one unnecessary nickel. By the time I finish here in three more years. I'll hopfully, have enough for a farm.

Do you like living in the country, Jane? Please say yes. You seem to blend into nature so beautifully.

I truly wish we could talk face to face. It is much better than the written, but please, keep the letters coming. I will live every day for them.

Until the next letter,

Yours truly, Thomas

Thomas wasn't as happy about college as his younger brother William, who was interested in medicine. Thomas liked the outdoors and working the farm and felt college a waste of time. He didn't want to be penned up in a building all day. However, he found he did like studying agriculture and was learning a lot of interesting things that would help him when he started farming. There were a lot of studies being done on growing better crops, such as the three sister's style used by the Indians. This was when you planted beans, corn, and squash all in one hill. The beans provided nutrients and the squash leafs held in the moisture and protected the soil, therefore resulting in a better crop of corn. He also was learning how to keep ledgers and records of how well the crops did. Machinery was being invented to make farming easier and Thomas would get first hand lessons on their use.

Jane read the letter with intense interest. Devouring every line and wrote him right back. By the time he received her second letter Jane was already moved into the finished room at the school. She wrote discribing to him the way she decorated her room so it suited her and how at home she already felt.

Dear Thomas,

I have moved into my own home. Though it is a very small space, I have managed to fit everything in. I have a small cupboard on one side of my bed and the comode on the other. Next to that is the door to the school room. There remains about a three foot space on the other side of the door in which I plan to put a rocking chair. In front of the bed there is space enough for a dresser. Your folks had an extra one with a mirror that I put in that space. On the other side of the room there is a cupboard where I'll keep my food and other odds and ends. Between the two there is another door that leads to the outside. I plan to braid a rug for in front of the door.

There is only one window that is on the left side of the room as you enter from the schoolroom. Directly across is a small opening cut into the wall so as to let in the heat from the fireplace. It doesn't seem to be enough to keep this room warm, but I guess I will find out this winter. However, I do have the luxury of the quilt that Ellen and Elizabeth made me before I left, which, I might add, brings hominess and brightness to the room. If the quilt doesn't keep me warm I will resort to the horse hair robe Hugh left. Just in case.

As for the chest that my folks so lovingly made for me, it will have to be put in the school room. It will go by the fireplace so I can have a place that is warm to sit and read.

I really enjoyed your letter and hope to receive another soon.

I greatly miss your company.

Affectionately, Jane

The quilt Elizabeth and Ellen had given Jane before they left home truly added color and warmth to her room. Ellen and Elizabeth made it from clothes that Ellen grew out of. They had worked on it while Jane was outside helping Hugh with the chores.

Helping Hugh with the chores was one thing Jane enjoyed doing with her step-father. They had built a relationship and understanding of each other during that time. Jane would miss those moments.

However, she was ready to move on.

She had just reread Thomas' letter for the third time. Her heart swelled and she fell into a dream state. She had, in fact, found herself daydreaming most of the time since receiving it.

It was still three weeks before school was in session, but Jane figured she had best get settled in and prepare for the future.

During the three weeks she had time to get better acquainted with the townfolks; although several families, whose children would be coming to school, came in from the country. Jane still had trouble matching the parent with child. In fact, most of the children in town hung out with each other, making it even harder to figure out who went with whom.

CHAPTER X

School and the Children

September had arrived quickly; almost too quickly for Jane. She was very nervous and didn't know what she was up against. Teaching school had always been her dream. For as long as she could remember she wanted to have a class of children, like Ellen, to teach and watch them grow into young adults. Jane's real mother always knew that some day she would be teaching and thought it a waste of knowledge if she didn't. Jane had a sudden twinge in her heart as her mother's image flickered on and off in her mind. Now Jane was standing in the door of her own school waiting for the first glimpse of the children to arrive.

Her thoughts were once again in the present and she felt her heart miss a beat as she spotted the wagon loaded to the hilt with the Lacy children laughing and waving her way. The wagon was being driven by their brother Thomas.

Thomas Lacy happened to be home from college, and was evidently, elected to drive his siblings to school. The wagon seemed to burst with the sound of children's voices, all excited for their first day back after the long summer. The girls were especially excited to have a lady teacher. The boys, although they liked Jane well enough, didn't know what to think, especially, the older ones. They were almost the same age as her and were already planning pranks. Thomas guided the team skillfully to a halt in front of the school not more than a few feet from where Jane was standing.

Thomas yelled a greeting. "Hello Jane. I figured I should come while I had a chance. Winter isn't very far off and I couldn't stand to think that it might snow and I wouldn't see you until spring."

The thought of not seeing Thomas for that long bothered Jane. Once winter had set in it would be hard to travel. Sometimes it would snow and people would be snowed in for the whole winter because the roads

<50>50</50>

would become trails and the trails were almost impassable. People knew the importance of being stocked up on provisions and having enough firewood to last several months.

Jane's eyes met Thomas' and locked. The kids were screaming and jumping off the wagon, heading for the school. "Thomas, what are you doing here? I just read your letter. You almost beat it here." Jane was so surprised to see Thomas she found herself saying whatever came to mind and not waiting for Thomas to answer.

Thomas was suddenly before Jane. He reached and grabbed her hand. His fingers stung Jane's as they touched.

"If all goes well I will try to come and visit during Christmas." Thomas promised.

After a much too short of a visit he turned back toward the wagon and was gone. Jane felt the burning in her fingers long after he had vanished down the road.

Jane turned and entered the school. The children's tables were lined up facing the desk in front. On the tables were slates with pieces of chalk on them, and a chair in front. There was a bell and other necessities on Jane's desk. She took a deep breath then slowly made her way across the room to escape into her tiny abode in back. In a panic, Jane closed the door so she could gather her strength.

She could hear the commotion getting louder and louder in the school room. Jane opened the door. It seemed she would never be able to handle that many children at once. She crossed the room and grabbed the bell setting on the corner of her desk and began ringing it. Everyone took heed and all found a place to sit. All accept one.

"Young man," Jane warned.

A boy of about twelve years old didn't hear, or acted like he didn't hear, anyway. He was busy writing nasty things about the girls on the black board.

"Young man," Jane repeated.

The boy was suddenly jolted from his intense job and turned with a startled look on his face saying, "I didn't do it! Honest I didn't!"

He had the most beautiful soft blue eyes that sparkled as he spoke. His blond hair was tousled and Jane could feel a bond as well as a challenge the minute their gazes met.

"What's your name, son?"

"Roy," he replied.

"I think you better take that chalk and start writing. 'I will not write bad things about the girls,' a hundred times."

Jane could hear him say, "oh boy," under his breath, as he dragged himself back to the blackboard and proceeded to write. This was the first of many writings of "I will nots," that Roy was to write.

Jane found that writing sentences on the blackboard, in front of the class, proved to be the most affective way of punishing the children. They hated to stand up at the black board and write sentences over and over. However, Roy was never able to resist an impulse and before he knew it he was in trouble.

While Roy wrote, Jane proceeded to arrange the children into rows by grade. John and Betsy were first grade so she put them up front. John Lacy was a quiet, blond haired youngster. His blue eyes were captivating and if he had been a busy type like Roy, Jane would have had a hard time punishing him. She had come to know him very well during her stay with the Lacys.

Betsy Curts had brown curly hair. She had it pulled back and held in place with two beautiful combs. Jane didn't think it would be hard for this little girl to take hold of her heart and be forever imbedded there.

This was to be true of all her children though, as Jane had come to think of them, and one day she would dread when they finished school and went out on their own.

David Curts was the only second grader. He had black hair, cut shoulder length, not as curly as his sisters, and his brown eyes seemed sad to Jane. It turned out David was having trouble learning to read. Jane came to take a special interest in helping him catch up.

Nine year old June Curts was the only fourth grader, and she was beautiful like her sister, and a very talkative child. She became Jane's number one helper and the one to keep her siblings in line. Even though, she could be a tomboy at other times, and loved to climb trees, and could outrun most of the boys in school.

Mary Curts was shy and withdrawn. She was a good child and an excellent student. She could pick up and retain instantly lessons not only given to her class, but she also listened to the other classes when they were up front getting instructions and retained everything she heard from those, too. If only she could come out of the shell she was in she would surely continue with higher education. Mary was old enough to remember an attack on their wagon. The men, who had assailed them, had beaten her father and raped her mother. In fact, David may have been the product of that assault. No one ever spoke about it. Stephen, their father, had never made mention of it and loved and treated David as his own. Mary, however, would always have scars from that incident.

Just about everyone in Jane's class had seen or been victims of a circumstance in their short lives. Jane tried to keep this in mind at all times when dealing with the children. She could relate to them and wanted to ease and erase all the bad memories from their minds. Although, Jane knew this would never happen, she made it her main goal to help the children realize that what had happened before would always be in the back of their mind, but the future was what they had to look forward to. If something bad happened, you must always remember there was still the future; the only thing left was to pick up the pieces and somehow continue on. Jane tried to go by these rules herself; however the memories would sometimes sneak up.

The Godspey children also had experienced a lot in their short lives. They were very young when they arrived at Brahman's Corner. They came from Massachusetts a couple of years after the Laceys.

Judith Godspey, age twelve, was the only fifth grader and although shy like Mary, once you got her to talk, she not only jabbered up a storm, but bounced the whole time she did so. She had green eyes and blond hair with a hint of red. She wore her hair in braids that her mother would pin up into a bun. Sometimes however, she would wear it down. It was thin and straight and never seamed to get tangled like naturally curly hair did.

Judith's brother, Lenny, a year older than his sister, had the same hair and eyes as Judith, but didn't have a shy bone in his body. He seemed to talk all the time. Jane was always pointing in his direction and shushing him. He was second in line to Roy with writing sentences, only his lines were, "I will not be disruptive by talking during class."

Abby Godspey, the oldest sister, had blond hair and light blue eyes and was the beauty of the classroom. All the boys, young or old, were caught staring at her. She always had a cheery smile on her face and seemed to enjoy life to its fullest. She would treat the other students well and if there was a problem to be resolved, Abby would be there to help solve it and maintain peace. She would be in the eighth grade, and that was as far as the classes went unless they could afford to go to the city to further their education.

Abner was named after his father and the only boy who had both an older sister as well as two younger ones. He thought that to be unfair. He had red hair, the same as his father and a million freckles on his face. He also had a temper to go with the red hair. He could have been a problem if it wasn't for his sisters. They seemed to be able to control his outbursts and to calm him down.

His cousin, Lenny, was eleven and not quite as energetic as Abner. He had the same color hair as him, although, his hair was a tangled mass of curls and his green eyes glistened with mischievousness. Lenny was small for his age. He was born with something wrong with his heart, they believed. He was always out of breath and tired. He couldn't run and play, like the other children. In spite of his frailty, he made it to school. He loved to read and bragged to have read the *Pilgrim's Progress* several times.

Justin was another reader and enjoyed school more than anything. His goal was to be a doctor and go to Harvard. Justin was always at school early. He said it was because he had a long way to go so left home early. His father, Josh Mathews, never socialized with the town folk and seemed to ignore anything his son did. Josh had lost his wife to influenza a few years back and hadn't been the same since. Justin became a very close friend of Jane's.

After Jane came to know the students and figured out their personalities, she had realized just how unique and important each and every one of them was. She enjoyed the mystery of solving these personalities. Just when she thought she would have one of them all figured out she would be surprised again. Day by day they changed and grew.

CHAPTER XI

Uncertain Future

Jane woke feeling refreshed and wondering even more why she had allowed herself to lose sight of all reality. She could feel the happiness she had in teaching the children and they were so vivid in her mind. She couldn't understand why she didn't follow her own rules on coping. Jane could only hope her memory fully returned and that she would again feel as wonderful as she did that morning. Jane looked up and saw her sister as she entered the room. She was such a beautiful young lady.

"Good morning, Ellen."

"Good morning to you, Jane. Your face is beaming and you look so vibrant this morning." Ellen was elated at seeing her sister as she improved day by day.

"That's because I've been remembering so many happy things. I had a dream about the kids and remember so many joyful times with them. What has happened to me, Ellen? What could be so bad that it stopped me from living?"

"I don't know, Jane, but I'm sure everything will come back and you will be okay."

"But what if I'm not, okay, Ellen? What if I go back into the state I was in? I'm frightened of what is buried inside my mind."

"I will do my best to keep you from falling back into that state, Jane. You know you can tell me anything. If you need someone to confide in, I will be here. Whatever happened to you was more than your mind could accept. It hurts me to think something that bad has happened to you. Together we will deal with it."

Jane and Ellen spent most of the day outside. They climbed the hill, took in the landscape, and relished the present, and enjoyed every second of that day together. After Jane helped Elizabeth with supper and dishes, she was exhausted and ready for a good night's sleep.

Jane fell into a deep sleep almost the minute her head hit the pillow; sleep that was unsettling. The memories weren't as soothing as the dreams from the night before. Sights and sounds were making there way into her mind. They were just flashes and they seemed to mean nothing to her. The picture that was most vivid was of a young man who was slovenly dressed with black tangled hair and an odor that caused Jane to suddenly be jolted awake. She was wet with perspiration and shaking uncontrollably. Who was this person, and why did he give her such a feeling of dread?

CHAPTER XII

Billy

"What's your name kid?" The stranger demanded as he kicked a boy who looked to be no more than sixteen.

"You know you don't belong on this property, don't you?" He gave the boy another boot. "I said, what's your name?"

The boy groaned and opened his eyes enough to see a tall lanky man with baggy pants held up with the aid of wide button on suspenders. His mouth was brown from the juice of a chew that he held in his lips. He drooled and slimy spit oozed from his mouth as he spoke.

"It's Billy, its Billy," stammered the boy, as his head struck against a rock on the ground where he lay.

"What's your full name?" Brown spit again spewed from the mouth of the stranger, sending splatters onto Billy's face.

Billy didn't remember ever hearing whether he had more than one name. However, he knew that the farmer where he had last found work had more than one. He tried to think quickly of a name when he noticed the remains of his supper and piped up, "Fisher, Billy Fisher." He groaned from another kick.

"I ain't ever heard of any Fisher family here' bouts. Where are you from?" Another stream of brown liquid zipped onto the ground once again missing the boy's head by a mere few inches.

Billy didn't know where he first lived. He only recalled certain incidents and flashbacks. He was having one now as the stranger picked up a large branch and held it over his head ready to club him. Billy suddenly sprang to his feet, grabbed a rock by his head on the way up and slammed it into the stranger's skull, sending him sprawling into the dirt. Then Billy was on top of him, beating his head over and over with the rock. All the while Billy was in another place, and the stranger was another person.

The man was really a stranger now. He had no face. Billy was a few feet away and saw nothing but a fog before him. He didn't know what had happened. He thought he was back at the cave with his mother, but there was no cave or no mother. Billy saw another flashback, it was his mother and there was someone on top of her, hurting her. Billy feared and hated this person. His mother was screaming. The brute was beating her. Suddenly Billy's mother was still; way too still. Billy started to run and run and run. This was so long ago yet it still hurt him and seemed like only yesterday.

Billy came back to the present, and saw what he had done. He rolled the body into a small concave, an obvious wash out from the last rain and buried the stranger to conceal him from the animals and anyone who might come looking for him. Then Billy picked up his blanket and fry pan and was once more in search of a home.

Billy had been living the last several years in the woods. He lived off rabbits by trapping them, a skill he had learned as a small child. This was the one thing he did well, trapping rabbits or any other small critter that he caught in the hand-made snares he built from small twigs. He would weave the twigs together with reeds until they were strong enough to capture his prey and this skill was what kept him from starving when far from another living soul.

Memories flashed through Billy's mind as he aimlessly wandered off, not sure where he would end up next.

As Billy walked on, his mind had opened and he saw vividly the man who hurt his mother. He remembered his mother saying, "This is your pa". He remembered how she had taught him how to survive on berries, and which weeds and herbs were good to eat that grew in the woods around their small dwelling; which was a dug out in the side of the river bank.

The cave served the purpose well. It was small, about five feet wide, by eight feet deep and only about four feet high. Billy's mother built a cover for the opening the same way she taught him to build snares; weaving sticks and reeds together. The man Billy was to call pa stayed only a few days that first time he met him, and Billy only saw him a couple of times after that, besides the time the man silenced his mother forever. And the man had beaten his mother those other times, too. The only real memory Billy had of his pa was him beating his mother. The last time Billy saw his mother alive, she had him hide somewhere in the woods for fear Billy's father would start beating him, too. Those memories had been hidden in Billy's mind for many years.

It was at that time, he left the only home he had ever known, and lived off the wilds of the forest. He didn't remember much after leaving home. He lost track of time. The last place Billy lived, however, he did remember. This was when his life belonged to the church and to Father Brink. Billy was taken in by him and had lived at the mission for two years. He had little recollection of his past and now it was flooding him.

Now he was trying to hide his past again.

After stumbling over downfall and brambles, Billy came upon a well traveled trail leading north and south. He chose the one going north. Billy had been walking for several days when the trail led into a clearing. To the left of the clearing was a small cemetery with wood and slate markers that had the names of the departed on them. Billy couldn't read any of the names though, because he could neither read nor write. Father Brick, back at the rectory, had tried to teach him but said he wasn't able to be taught anything. He was stupid.

There was a hill leading down to a creek from where Billy stood. It was a beautiful and peaceful spot. He sat down and leaned back against a tree and took in all the sights and sounds of serenity. Billy wished it would be like this forever, but figured the only way that could happen was if he were resting beneath one of those markers. He saw the trail that he was taking led him through a small line of trees and brush.

Billy forced himself up, weak from hunger and days of walking through underbrush, and started on his way again. He didn't go more than twenty feet when he came upon another clearing. On this piece of land was built a small wooden structure; maybe a school or perhaps a church. There was a cloths line stretched across from the building to an elm tree. It was a little ways from the edge of the wooded area that divided the cemetery from the clearing where the structure sat.

There, at the clothsline hanging sheets was a woman. Billy thought her to be the most beautiful women he had ever seen. Her black hair was blowing in the wind as were the sheets. She was struggling to get them over the line, dividing them in half so they didn't blow right back off again. Her long dress was billowing from her slender waist emphasizing the fullness of her breasts. Billy was instantly aroused. He knew what that was, because the boys from the mission told him all about it. Billy stood there as still as possible watching.

Then the woman looked up and spotted him. He instantly lowered his head and turned to go back the way he had just come.

"Hello." The voice was as beautiful and soft as she looked.

Billy stopped and slowly turned back around. "Hi." His voice caught in his throat. The words were stuck tight and he couldn't seem to speak. Billy stammered even worse than he did when he was being kicked by the stranger.

"I'm Jane, I teach school here. Are you lost?"

He wasn't only lost, but he was also hungry. He was dirty; his hair was long and tangled and stiff from many days with out washing or brushing. The blood from hitting his head on the rock was dried and crusted. His cloths had holes in them and there was blood spatters all over him.

"No, I'm looking for a work." Billy was moving from foot to foot as if ready to run.

"What is your name?" Jane asked.

"Billy," he replied.

"Have you had anything to eat today?"

"No ma'am." Father Brinks had said it was proper to say ma'am when addressing a young lady, remembered Billy. He was fidgeting and shuffling his feet as he answered her.

"I have some cold oatmeal left over from breakfast if you would like some."

Billy shyly walked over to the building; Jane stepped aside for him as he entered the cool interior. He noticed a couple of lines of tables and chairs straight ahead, and as they walked inside there was a large oak desk on the right side of the room and a small table with about four chairs on the left side.

Jane motioned for the boy to sit at the big desk, and then she went into the room in back of the school for the food.

While she was gone Billy took in the surroundings. The desk he sat at was a square oak table with one drawer and a captain's chair. There were several books stacked to one side of the table and a stack of smaller writing slates with several pieces of chalk by them. There was a bell that he figured was used to summon the children when recess was over, because it looked the same as the one Father Brink had. The tables in front of him were long and closer to the floor; the benches made to fit. On the wall to the left of him was a black-board going all the way across the middle of the wall. There was a ledge across the bottom that held the pieces of chalk. There was scribbling on the blackboard and that was all it was to Billy, scribbling. There was a fireplace in the back corner of the building and a kettle of water sat on the hearth. Billy's thoughts were interrupted as the far door was opened and the lady stepped into the room. Billy's heart began to race uncontrollably.

Jane brought Billy some cereal and a thick slice of bread spread with freshly churned butter that the Lacy children had brought the day before. Thinking of the Lacy's had caused Jane's mind to wonder to Thomas, which in turn had brought a smile to her face. Billy squirmmed uneasily and beamed at her thinking the smile was intended for him.

"I think she likes me," thought Billy.

Once again his desire made him squirm.

"I think Reverend Bogert, somtimes, can use a hand over at the rectory." Jane said.

"I'll have to stop and s-see," stammered Billy.

Billy took his time savoring each bite he took. He watched as Jane was folding some clothes she had brought in earlier. Whenever she looked his way he would bow his head to avoid eye contact. Billy suddenly slid his chair back, startling Jane.

Billy grinned at Jane as he said goodbye. Jane raised her hand and watched as he left; her mind still was far away thinking of Thomas.

Billy walked toward town. He thought he had fallen in love. And he was sure that Jane felt the same for him. About a mile from the school he came to the edge of town and the first building he encountered was a church.

Billy walked up to the door and stuck his head in. The room wasn't that much bigger than the school except it had a much steeper ceiling. The pews were in several rows on each side of the room. He slowly walked up the isle toward the pulpit. There was no one around.

"Hello, is anyone here?" His voice resounded throughout the room.

There was no answer so Billy went back outside and there coming up the trail from the outhouse was the Reverend. At least Billy presumed it was the Reverend because he was dressed in black, like Father Brink.

"Hello, I'm Billy and I'm wondering if you might have some work for me. I will work for a place to sleep and eat." Billy once again was stepping from one foot to the other as he spoke.

Reverend Bogert looked Billy up and down. He couldn't remember seeing him around here before and couldn't decide if he liked the lad or not. However, he looked so helpless he decided it would be only right to take him in.

"I guess I do have a few chores you can do. The Reverend replied. Can you sweep? There are some weeds and grass that needs to be cut. Can you use a scythe?" The Reverend was suddenly finding all kinds of things he could use the boy for.

"You can start right away if you want."

Reverend Bogert handed Billy a scythe and showed him where to start cutting. Billy had never used a scythe before but was able to figure it out. At first Billy was a little wild and almost hit the Reverend in the leg. The Reverend stayed away after that and trusted Billy with the job. Reverend Bogert was happy to get out of that ugly chore. He was happy to get out of any chore, for that matter.

Billy not only began doing chores for the Reverend, he also did odd jobs for other businesses and other churches in town. Billy was a good worker, and even though he was a loner and no one knew where he stayed most nights, people thought him harmless.

Actually, Billy lived in the woods. He had discovered a spot on the other side of the cemetery across from where the school sat. This way he could sneak over to the thicket across from the cemetery and see if Jane was outside hanging clothes or doing yard work. Jane wasn't aware that Billy was watching everything she did while she was outside. He was too shy to talk to her, and never seemed to get up the nerve to do so no matter how he tried. He was very skillful at staying hidden.

When Billy went to and from town he took the wooded area along the river passing the clearing where the school and cemetery were. That way he was always out of sight and the area was rugged enough nobody ever went that way. He had found a cave in the riverbank where he did as his mother had done; weaved a door out of small branches and reeds that camouflaged his home, his hideout.

Billy had known by this time his desire for the woods. He tried to stay at the rectory and did so every now and then when it was cold or stormy weather. But he liked his cave and being in the woods better. It made him feel he was close to Jane. He dreamed she loved the woods too.

Billy would watch her through the trees while she hung her clothes. "I wonder if she needs any help," he thought. He wished he could bring himself to walk up to her and ask. Billy jerked his head and bumped into a tree branch. All of a sudden Jane stopped what she was doing and looked around. Billy quickly stepped back into the thicket.

Billy thought he either needed to stop hiding and confront Jane with his feelings for her or he would get caught, and he knew that it wouldn't be good. Billy waited a few minutes, and then scampered back to his home.

Billy didn't know why nobody ever discovered where he stayed. He wasn't trying to be invisible to anyone, except Jane. He even had a small fire at night. He supposed it was because he was down the embankment far enough that he was hidden from view.

Billy never cooked anything there because he got his meals at the rectory, so the only reason for a fire was for warmth and it made him feel more like when he was with his mother. Billy missed his mother now that he remembered her. He didn't remember why he had blocked out his past life. The last thing he remembered before the rectory was a farm he lived at. He didn't even remember how he came to be there. The farmer, Mr. Jeneky, was a brute though.

Mr. Jeneky was a huge fellow that wore pants that hung down below his bay window and were held there with suspenders. He always wore a plaid flannel shirt with several missing buttons that revealed dingy grey underwear. He had a bald head that would burn and peal and turn brown in the summer. He would wham Billy on the head and bellowed out orders to him. Billy was just small at the time. He didn't remember how long he was there. However, he remembered the day he left.

He knew he had grown older, bigger, and stronger while at Mr. Jeneky's. One day Mr. Jeneky was whipping him and yelled at him to work faster at pitching manure out of the barn door. Billy saw red, and turned on Mr. Jeneky with the pitchfork. Then he ran for days and days once again living off nature until he stumbled on the mission.

Billy had a pretty good existence while at the mission. Even though father Brink always referred to him as stupid, he always had food in his belly and a warm place to sleep. However, Billy knew when it was time to move on.

CHAPTER XIII

Fourth of July Celebration

The horror Jane had felt about the ragged boy made her want to hide and not to be seen by anyone. She was cold and there was a foreboding that lingered long after she awoke. Jane knew the memories must flow to heal completely, and only hoped she was able to bear what was to come. She felt this was the part of her memory that was buried in her mind. She felt sick to her stomach and sat on the edge of the bed sobbing silently. She forced herself to her feet and out to the other room, then stoked the fire to heat some water for tea. Once calm, she made her way back to bed. This time when Jane slept and she found herself back with the children and doing what she loved most.

—∞◦⊰◉⊱◦∞—

Jane could hardly believe how quickly the winter went. She made it through the first year of teaching without pulling out any of her hair. She truly loved teaching. The children seemed to feel about her as she did them.

As Jane walked through town, thinking of the children, she heard someone calling her name.

"Miss Jane! Miss Jane! Hello! Miss Jane." It was Roy; his hair was tousled, and smudges of dirt were on his face. He was walking his horse through town.

"Hello. Are you enjoying the summer?"

"You bet I am. I've been getting ready for the race next month."

Everyone waited anxiously for the Fourth of July, a celebration that had gone on every year since the ending of the revolution. Last year the first place winner received ten dallors. This year it's going to be twenty-five. People came from all around for the race. Dave Adams won last year.

64

"I hope I win this year."

Jane could see that Roy was already imagining what he would spend his winnings on, even though; it was the win, not the money that he wanted.

"I hope you do too, Roy." She couldn't help but laugh out loud.

"My horse is getting anxious to run. He loves running and can go on forever without tiring. I think this will help me win."

Roy was so excited he couldn't seem to hold still. His horse was as ready as he was. He got on his horse, waved at her, gave his steed a kick, and galloped up the path, over the hill and out of sight. Something he had done many times for two weeks. He would take the same road every time. It was the same route the race was on. Jane cheered as he bolted ahead and then she headed on into town.

Jane was smiling as she entered the mercantile. Harriet was busy helping her sister-in-law stock the shelves. She turned with a grin. "Hi Jane, you look happy."

Jane chuckled but contained her laughter enough to tell Harriet how Roy was determined to win the big race.

"It wouldn't surprise me if he does. He has the will power and takes his horse out every day. It is the one thing that he does that keeps him out of mischief." Harriet was proud of her son and loved him dearly, even though he was a handful.

"I hope to have a son like Roy someday, Harriet. I know it could be a challenge, but it would also be rewarding. You are so lucky." Jane said

Thomas suddenly came into her thoughts and Jane once again was dreaming of a future with him. She hardly remembered gathering the supplies she needed.

Thomas Lacy would be home a couple of days during the summer and one of those would be Independence Day. He was in Jane's thoughts all the time. It seemed they had so much to catch up on, and what time they did have together was too short.

Jane wouldn't have gotten through some of the days if it weren't for the children keeping her busy in the winter and Jessica coming home for the summer. Jessica and Jane had become close friends, and when Jessica and Dave married last fall and moved to a place in the country, Jane knew she would be missing a very dear friend. Dave and Jessica had been in town several times already that spring and when it was close to Jessica's due date, Jessica would come back to Duanesburg to stay with her father for a few weeks. Jessica wanted Jane to be there to help with the delivery.

Jessica was radiant since her and Dave married, and being pregnant with his baby, she was almost smothered with happiness. Jessica would go to Jane's a couple of hours every evening.

Jane was helping sew a layette for the baby. She could see Jessica in the distance. Jane stepped outside and waved a greeting.

"Good evening! Jessica."

"Hello! Jane."

Jane went to meet her and they walked back to the school chattering all the way. You would have thought they hadn't seen each other for days; when in fact, they had been together the night before.

"What are we making for the baby tonight, Jessica?"

"I would like you to help me put the bindings on a couple of baby quilts. It goes so much quicker when two people sew; one on each end of the quilt. I don't know what I would do if I didn't have you to help me with all this extra sewing."

"I know two people are better than one, Jessica, said Jane. When Elizabeth got to the binding on her quilts she would always have me help. As for me helping you, I have plans including you when I get to the binding on a quilt I'm making."

"I am all too happy to help you with it, Jane. I owe you so much already."

"You don't owe me anything Jessica. I have enjoyed every minute I have spent helping you get ready for the baby. In fact, the only payment I expect from you is you having me help with the baby. I can hardly wait until it arrives."

"Me either, Jane, I so want to be holding it in my arms."

"What do you want, a boy or a girl, Jessica?

"I hope it is a son for Dave. I don't care what it is, but I sense Dave would really like a boy."

"In that case, I hope you have a boy too, said Jane. Although wouldn't it be nice to make some little girl clothes?"

"Yes, it would," beamed Jessica, as she thought about the possibilty of a little girl.

It was a nice spring evening so they decided to work outside. They brought out a couple of chairs and sat facing each other.

The back of the quilt was made of soft cotton muslin and Jane noticed that the material on the top was bits and pieces of a couple of Jessica's old dresses.

The evenings Jessica and Jane had spent together sewing were times they would cherish. They were true friends. Jane was glad Jessica and Dave had married. He was so good to her. It was because of this union, that Jessica and Jane were brought together. Dave's friendship was one that she would always hold dear, and Jane felt the same closeness to Jessica.

The memories that were flooding in Jane's mind lately were sweet and made her wonder what could possibly have been so bad she wanted them erased. She would spend every afternoon talking with Ellen. Telling her about the children and how close she and Jessica had become. Jane thought of Jessica and her wish for a boy. She felt a sudden forbodding thinking of Jessica. As though something had happened that Jane wasn't aware of. She almost gathered up enough nerve to ask Elizabeth, then for some reason didn't.

"Ellen, why did you decide to move to Albany?"

"Because I plan to get the rest of my education in Scotland and thought it wise to test my strength to see whether I could stay away from home for a long period of time. As it is I get so homesick now and hope to get over it by next year because that is when I am parting for Scotland."

Ellen sounded excited about the prospect of going abroad. Jane felt a pang in her heart thinking of her sister going so far away. They visited most of the afternoon. Yet Jane felt she was missing a huge part of her life.

Jane and Ellen spotted Elizabeth out the window and decided to go out and help her in the garden. It seemed that she was having more and more difficulty in doing her daily chores.

"Mother, let us do this." Ellen insisted that her mother take a break while they finished weeding.

"Yes Mother, you need to take it easier. You are wearing yourself out." Jane took Elizabeth by the arm and guided her to a bench that Hugh had built and put at the end of the garden so his wife could rest every so often while she worked.

Jane and Ellen worked about an hour. At that time the garden looked great.

They went over to the bench and sat down by Elizabeth.

Jane was the first to speak. "Mother, what happened to me? I am ready to know."

Elizabeth told Jane how they had found her when they had gotten to Duanesberg. "That is all I know. I hope that once you figure it out you will tell us."

Jane's mind began openning a little everyday. It seemed that it was while she slept that the memories unfolded. Her thoughts were always taken back to the school and her children. Jane wondered what happened to them. She felt that she deserted them.

CHAPTER XIV

A New School Year

It was the start of a new school year. Jane had taught in Duanesburg for a little over a year. She was looking forward to seeing the children's shinny faces and their eager and energetic selves ready to help whenever needed. Jane could count on Justin, the oldest, to be at school ahead of all the other children. He rode his horse several miles to get to the school and was always there offering to help.

"Miss Jane!" Jane could hear him yelling her name as he entered the front door. "Miss Jane, are you there?"

Jane yelled back, "I'm over here Justin." Jane was about to move her desk into the corner of the room and was standing where he couldn't see her.

"Can you give me a hand, Justin?"

Justin loved to help and was there at the drop of a hat.

"Are you glad to be back at school, Justin?"

"Yes, it's great to be out of the fields and where I can read all I want." He said as he guided the desk into place.

"This is your last year, isn't it?"

"Yes, it is. Should I fill the water bucket while I'm at it?" asked Justin.

"Sure, but wait a minute, what are your plans after this year?"

Justin stopped and was deep in thought for a moment.

"I would like to go to medical school. I don't know how I'm going to manage it but that is what I want."

"Have you ever talked with William Lacy? He's in medical school somewhere in Massachusetts. Harvard, I believe."

"I only know the Lacys that come to school here; however, I would like to meet William. Could you possibly arrange a meeting for me?"

"I will be seeing Thomas sometime the end of December and I'll see if it can be arranged. William may be home for Christmas. I know that Thomas will be."

"Thank you, Miss Jane; I really appreciate all the help." Justin then grabbed the bucket and went out to the well for water.

Thoughts of Thomas would stick in Jane's mind from the time his name was mentioned. They were becoming so close. Over the Fourth of July they were together, and Jane wanted him to stay. She wished he lived closer, but was content with what little time she had with him. It was at that time he first asked Jane to marry him and come to Massachusetts. He felt she could easily find a position in Albany. However, Jane wanted to finish out one more year here before she made that big of a decision. And besides, she had felt they really didn't know each other well enough. Even though, it had been over a year since they met, they were actually together only a few of those days. Jane knew there were strong feelings between them, but for the moment this would have to do.

Thomas came to town a couple of times during the summer, and each time he was insistent on marriage. Jane held back. She wanted to prove to herself that she could live on her own. Thomas' one thought was to take care of her. Jane couldn't believe she had only known Thomas a little over a year and yet knew him to be the man she wanted to be the father of her children, and live her life with. When Thomas was away at college he wrote her often, and she would sometimes get more than one letter at a time, because when someone would have go to the city they would bring the mail back with them. Even though the mail was slow Jane looked forward to them.

While Justin was busy Jane went back to her living quarters. She saw the rug in front of the back door was in need of dusting. Picking it up, she stepped outside to shake out the dirt. Suddenly she looked up and glanced over her small backyard, which was a clearing of half grown grass that was starting to brown with the coming of fall, and the huge elm that stood at the right of her home was turning yellow with streaks of red. There were yellow black-eyed susans and white daisies peaking through the waving brown grass. Next, Jane's eyes followed the path that lead to a line of young trees. Behind this thicket she could just bearly make out some of the small slabs used to mark the graves The cemetery always gave her an eerie feeling and sometimes she wished she was closer to town. She should be accustomed to the cemetery by now, but still felt the same about it as she did the first time she noticed it. Although, Jane didn't find herself looking into that direction every time she opened her back door like she had the first few months she was there.

However, that time Jane shivered, finished dusting the rug, and went back inside. She could hear more children arriving. As she left her room; she couldn't help but smile as she watched the children laughing and yelling, excited to be back visiting with their friends.

"Good morning. Miss Jane."

"Good morning children."

The first day back was always the most exciting for the children. To see the happiness in their faces when they first saw their friends, some they hadn't seen in a while, was so satifying to Jane. She waited for them catch up on all the fun they had during the summer, then rang the bell summoning that it was time to get started with the lessons.

First, Jane called off their names to see if everyone made it to school. Jane taught eight grades of classes, because by the eighth grade, the kids would have finished what education they needed and either started working or they would be ready to move to the city to continue with their learning. However, some of the children couldn't afford to live away from home so she would let those that wanted to continue, attend school there. Most of the children from the country would never be able to move so far off, not only for financial reasons, but also because their folks needed their help at home. Jane realized that there would come a day when there would be too many children and she would have to quit doing this. She saw she had three extra children this year. Glancing at her list she realized one person was missing.

Everyone was there except for Roy. Like Justin was always the first one to school, Roy was the last. He always came shuffling in, usually a little late, with his hair a mess and clothes in disarray. Roy lived on the far edge of town and was always distracted on his way to school. His folks were insistent that Roy get an education because neither of them had any kind of schooling. They knew little in the way of a trade, and even less about farming. When speaking with Roy's parents, Jane noticed that Josh Herk, Roy's father, seemed to be slow and withdrawn.

Because of this, Josh Herk took whatever odd jobs available to support his family. Right now Roy's uncle, Andrew Herk, was using his brother to help unload and stock supplies at the mercantile. This was only a couple of days work a week. Not enough to raise a family. Roy was Josh Herk's, only child. One knew very little about this family, because even though Andrew was the out-spoken one of the family, he never talked about their personal life.

Josh was thankful his brother and sister-in-law gave them work, and to the town's people who would bring him garden vegetables, during the season. When some of the farmers came to town with milk or cream they made sure to supply his family with what they could spare; also, was the case with meat. Because of this generosity and Roy liking to hunt and often bringing in a rabbit or grouse for supper, the family seemed to get along fine.

The life the Herks led before they came to Duanesburg was unknown to anyone in town. Everyone presumed their life to have been harsh. They both seemed to be looking over their shoulders and jumpy. Both brothers had permanent scars on their faces, and what you could see, of their arms. The people of town never questioned them about their scars because they figured them to be from the war. Josh had a huge scar at the top of his forehead, probably the cause of his being simple.

They were church going and very honest. Roy's mother Harriet, was soft spoken, very shy and withdrawn. She did the best she could raising Roy. However, Roy was overactive and hard for her to control. She loved her son and always seemed gentle with him. Jane never saw any signs of beatings or harsh treatment like she saw once on one of the other children. Jane had visited her family the next day and hopefully put a stop it. Jane believed in spankings and firm discipline, but leaving bruises and welts was more than she could take. Roy's father was also gentle with Roy. Josh always talked softly to his son, even when Jane would have probably pulled his ear and sent him to the corner; something she had done more than once during the last school year. Jane was wondering how he would be to handle this year, as Roy came in slamming the door behind him.

"Hello, Miss Jane!" he yelled.

"Hello, where have you been?"

"I got side-tracked. My horse wanted to see what was going on down at the other end of town. So I let him. It was nothing but a scuffle going on between two of the O'Neal kids. I cheered for the little one, and he won too, Miss Jane."

Roy was so excited he hopped from foot to foot as he related his story.

The O'Neals quit sending their kids to school because they needed them to help at home. They were only fourteen and fifteen years old. They were both small for their age.

"The oldest kid, Tom, tripped over his own pant leg and fell, giving the advantage to his younger brother; the little rascal jumped on top and started pounding him. Father Joseph had to grab him by the scruff of his neck and haul him off. You never saw the like, Miss Jane."

Roy liked excitement and probably wished he was one of them involved in the fighting. Jane had to take him by the shoulders and hold him hold until he calmed down. The other kids were getting as excited as Roy and wanted to go and see the excitement. There was an ear-deafening humdrum with the mixture of kids' voices and the scuffling sounds of them sliding their chairs. They were ready to head for the other end of town.

"Settle down!" Jane yelled.

She released her hands from Roy's shoulders and raised them to halt the exit.

"Please can we go see? Miss Jane." There was a chorus of voices as the children all yelled at once.

"It's all over, and time for class. So sit down. Matilda, you may pass out the slates. Marie you may pass out the chalk. Everyone else, go to your seats and sit down. The excitement is over."

Soon all one could hear were the slates and chalk being placed on the tables in front of the children. Jane had their assignments already on the black board so the children were kept busy while she brought the individual classes to the table in front for discussion. Jane always started with the first and second grades and then the next one after that until she got through each one.

Everything went well for the rest of the morning. The children went outside to play during lunch time. Jane could hear laughter and yells from the kids as they chased after each other trying to be the one to tag the most people for the chosen team. You would think they were in a real battle by the way they put all of their energy into what they were trying to accomplish, and run until they were completely out of breath. They were having so much fun, and it was such a beautiful day, that Jane let them play an extra fifteen minutes. Still, when she rang the bell for them to come in she heard a steady drone of, "oh, do we have toos." Jane guessed they were still wound up from the morning excitement. They all came dragging in. Surprisingly Roy was the first one, and he was actually sitting down. The one thing that Jane didn't see was the string that ran from his seat to the door. However, one of the girls did and picked it up and started to roll it up. All of a sudden there came a yowl of pain from Roy as he grabbed the string and pulled it toward him.

"Let go! Let go! Let go!" He yelled over and over.

Jane ran to his aid, only to be astonished and angry at the same time. Roy had the string attached to his penis as a joke. However, the joke was on him.

Jane couldn't think of any, "I will not do any more," sentences for this action, so decided to keep him after school and walked him home so he could explain the reason he was in trouble to his folks.

The day went fast. Roy thought that Jane forgot that she would be walking him home. He managed to sneak out and was about to sprint off when he heard.

"Roy, you wait for me."

Roy stopped dead in his tracks and waited for Jane to catch up.

"Do I have to tell my parents?"

"I think this to be the only way to make you understand you have to think before you do things, Roy."

"I promise I will from now on, Miss Jane."

"That's good Roy. However, I think this is one time you need to explain your actions to your parents."

Roy's shoulders slumped. Jane wished she could take him in her arms and tell him it would be okay. They reached the Herk's and Jane waited until Roy finished telling the reason for the escort home.

Josh Herk turned to Jane and asked. "What shall we do about this? I know Roy needs to be punished. Do you have any suggestions?"

Jane looked around and saw there was a wagon of supplies that Josh was unloading for his brother.

"How about unloading the wagons for you for a couple of days; as a steady reminder to him why he is doing it?"

Josh looked at Roy and said, "You better get started Roy."

Roy started to unload the wagon. Jane thought he was relieved that this was his punishment, because he probably thought he surly warranted a beating for doing such an awful deed.

The rest of the year Roy's behavior was acceptable. He seemed to be maturing into a handsome young man. He was still a little mischievous, and Jane hoped that never changed. The twinkle in his eyes when he could get a rise out of someone was what was most attractive about him. Jane found that whenever there was a lot of laugher coming from the children, it seemed, Roy was the center of the attention. Jane's one hope was to keep him going in the right direction.

CHAPTER XV

Good Times

Jane couldn't believe how fast the winter went by. The kids were wonderful. It was hard for her to imagine that two whole school years had come and gone. She knew teaching would be her future. She already missed the kids. Jane would be losing two children this year and gaining three. Mary and Matilda would be through with their education. They would be replaced by Mary's sister Betty Curts and Matilda's brother John Lacy. Andrew Jones, son of Joseph and Sally Jones, would also be attending. Joseph owned a small flour mill outside of town. Jane's school family was growing.

Jane saw some of the kids off and on during the summer. Justin still came to check up on her now and again, and she saw the Lacy children whenever they came into town with their folks.

Jane got to be good friends of the Jones'. With Jessica and Dave so far away, it was nice to have someone to take their place. She really missed Jessica. However, Sally became a great friend, too. She and her husband lived about a mile from the school and Jane walked to visit Sally a couple of times a week. It was a nice hike. She would take the cut off Sally's husband, Joseph, had cleared through the woods. It made the journey to town for his wife and himself a little shorter.

Sally was married at sixteen, which was quite common, especially when you came from a large family. Sally was the oldest of ten children when she left home to be married, she looked way to young and tiny to have a six year old.

Jane watched how Sally took care of her son and made sure everything was neat and tidy for them. It made the sudden burst of maternal instinct in Jane strong and realized that she was getting to the age when people thought of a woman as an old spinster.

Joseph was good to Sally and his adoration was obvious. Joseph was ten years older and owned the property he farmed several years before he married. They had a nice two bedroom cabin. The living area was large and comfortable. Jane and Sally would get together and sew quilts like Jane had done with Jessica. Jane would feel a twinge of guilt sometimes. She missed her friend dearly.

Jane sat on the cabin floor with Sally working on the second quilt that week.

"It looks like we will have a couple of quilts ready to sell at the 4th of July celebration."

The plan was to try and make several different items to sell. They had already made several braided rugs and now would have two quilts to sell besides.

"Do you think anyone will need a quilt and actually buy one, Jane?" Most people made their own clothing and quilts.

"We won't know until we try, Sally. If we don't, we'll each have an extra one."

Jane and Sally had visited and worked until late in the afternoon. It was time for Jane to go home. It would be daylight for a little while yet, but Jane knew if she didn't leave now they would get to talking again and forget the time.

"Stop in for lunch the next time you and Joseph come to town."

"We would love to, Jane."

Jane turned and waved again before she started down the path that led through the woods.

Jane was fearless of the woods and loved to look for blueberries and other berries that were in season. She picked what she needed to make jams and jellies that she shared with the children during the school year. There was a clearing about a half mile into the woods that had a hill in the middle. Some days on her way to the Jones' she would climb to the top and lie in the tall grass and dream of a future, and Thomas was always a part of those dreams.

Every once in a while, she would get the sensation that she was being watched, but she never saw anyone.

Billy always stayed a short distance back, making sure that he wasn't seen. Because of his Indian upbringing he was able to keep hidden and could sneak through the woods without making any noise. Although a couple of times he thought he was spotted.

Billy still hadn't gotten up the courage to tell Jane what he felt about her. He would dream of how he would save her if she was to come into danger. It's been two years now and he still stammered when he spoke to her. His dreams seemed to be coming more and more real. Every time he decided to tell her his feelings he would wait one more week. That one more week turned into two years.

Jane still smiled and talked to him in passing. Billy was always eager when reverend Bogert wanted him to deliver a message to Jane or one of the children. Nobody ever took the time to talk to Billy as Jane did.

CHAPTER XVI

Summer Vaction

Jane missed Thomas. Even though he had been there every weekend since the beginning of June, and that had been the last three weekends, it still wasn't often enough. Last weekend he asked Jane again to come back to Albany with him. He told her she could work there teaching as well as in Duanesburg. After one more year Thomas would graduate and be ready to start farming. Jane felt they could wait one more year.

Still Thomas was persistent. "Please, Jane, I want you near me. Would you to be my wife? Please say yes." Thomas was eager for Jane to respond.

"I want so much to be your wife, but I'm not ready to leave my job or my children. It is what I always wanted and I am so much at home in Duanesburg. The kids love me as I love them. Besides I am afraid of making such a big move. And what if being a woman I don't find a postion. I'm sorry, Thomas, I feel as you do, but I think we should wait until you finish school. It isn't good to rush into things. I know you have dreams and if we hurry into this to fast it could ruin everything you have dreamed of."

"Right now you are all that's in my dreams, Jane," Thomas answered.

His eyes melted into Jane's as he spoke. Jane felt faint with passion. Thomas leaned over and kissed her. Their lips tingled and burned as they touched.

"I don't mean or want to rush you. I'll be here whenever you are ready to take that step." Thomas stepped away from Jane. The rest of the time they were together they spent visiting and discussing their future.

It had been a week since Thomas went back to Albany and Jane could still feel his presence. She thought she just might have to give in and go with him. Thomas wouldn't be back until the Fourth of July, celebration, which seemed like an eternity to Jane.

Independence Day was the biggest celebration of the year. People came from miles around to watch the horse races and all the other contests, such as the three legged race, the gunny sack race, and all the other relay races that the kids participated in.

Of course, the horse race was the event of the year. Dave and Jessica would be there for sure. Jane could hardly wait to see them. She hadn't seen them in almost a year at which time she helped as Jessica gave birth to a robust baby boy. They called him Davy after his father; however, they planed to have an Indian naming ceremony for him this summer while they were still close to the reserve. Dave's people didn't give their children their Indian names until they were a year old. Davy's Indian name would be Thunder.

Jessica had told Jane she was learning the ways of her husband's people and wanted to understand those customs, because she felt they were something she could teach their son. She wanted Davy to know both of his parent's way of life.

Dave found good and bad amongst the whites as well as the Indians. He wanted Jessica to become familiar with his culture; however, he decided to buy a farm that was midway between Duanesburg and the Indian village.

It was actually closer for them to go to Fort Niagara than to Duanesburg. However, they planned to be here for the horse race on the fourth of July, not only because of his wife's family being here, but also because Dave never missed the horse race. Dave had won the money last year. He and Jessica could use the money and Dave was quite sure he would have no problem winning again.

Of course, Roy was certain that he would win this year. He had raced last year and came in second. He had been training for the race all spring and was determined to come in first this year. Every day Jane saw him as he galloped by on his pet and companion of the last three years. His horse's name was Lightning. Jane hoped he would be the big winner this year. He tried so hard. Jane realized that Dave and Jessica needed the money; but Roy needed the win. Not only did he need it for the thrill, he also needed it to build his confidence. She could imagine the sparkle in Roy's eyes if he were to win.

"Yee haw!"

The loud voice and the thundering of hooves were once again flashing by, as Roy galloped past the school full speed ahead to the top of the knoll and out of sight. Jane felt that she had been at the race for the hundredth time since the beginning of summer. She laughed as she raised her hand to greet him and cheered him on.

Jane had just received a letter from Thomas. He was saying that he had to work the day before the fourth and didn't think he would be able to make it for the day time festivities, but would be there for sure to escort her to the dance. Jane didn't care as long as she saw him. It was still a week before the fourth and it seemed a long way off.

Independence Day had finally arrived. It was a nice sunny day after a three day rain. The ground was soft and muddy. Jane hoped that it wouldn't cause any problems for the race. The road being taken was always full of potholes, and was more of a trail than a road, anyway.

It was noon and all of the townspeople were gathered on Main Street. Jane slowly made her way through the crowd and to the starting place for the race. It was a difficult task, since everyone wanted to stop and talk. Jane finally made it just as the horses and riders were lining up. Jane spotted Dave and Roy in the lineup, and they both raised there hands in greeting. Roy was beaming when he saw her.

The men on horseback were anxiously waiting for the sharp sound of the revolver. The pistol exploded and the horses took off thundering down the road. Jane was cheering, this time for real, as the riders sped by. Dave Adams and Roy were neck and neck. They jumped out ahead and were a horse length in front of the other riders in the first few seconds. Before long they were out of sight. There were people located at several spots along the route. Some of them had run ahead trying to take in as much of the race as possible. Jane decided to stay put and take in some of the exhibits.

Jane turned and spoted Dave's wife, Jessica. She was standing by her father, Parson Jones. Their eyes met and the next thing you knew they were heading toward each other. Beside her and hanging tightly to Jessica's hand, was the cutest little boy Jane had ever seen. He had a beautiful round face, with the chubbiest cheeks. He had a thick mass of black hair. It didn't seem possible that he had grown so big and was walking.

He squirmed when Jane picked him up to give him a hug. Her maternal instincts once again took over. She almost decided then and there to tell Thomas she would marry him.

"How is it being a mom, Jessica?"

"I love it Jane. It was hard at first, but Dave helped me break into the life of motherhood. He is such a good husband and father. He can make little Davy laugh by just looking at him."

The baby was so soft and cuddly; Jane wanted to hold on to him forever. Davy didn't know her and was content for only a short time. He spotted his mother and his little arms were out-stretched for her. Jane was so happy for Jessica and her new life.

As Jessica and Jane were catching up on the time they had been apart they heard and saw a commotion by the starting line.

Jane hurried over to see what was going on only to find Dave carrying a limp body in his arms. She knew before she got there that it was Roy. Her heart was racing as she reached Dave's side. There was a sudden cry from the crowd.

"What did he do?"

Jane knew they were talking about Dave. Dave turned to her and asked if she knew where Jessica was.

"She's with her father." Jane's voice quivered as she struggled to keep her emotions under control.

"Things will get out of hand, Jane. I'm going to have to leave. Tell Jessica I'll be back and I love her."

Dave then gently put Roy's limp body on the ground. He mounted his horse and galloped out of sight going into the dense forest, knowing, that his heritage would bring him injustice, but it would also help in his survival. He heard the screams of Roy's mother as he disappeared from sight.

"What did he do to my boy? What did that Indian do to my son?"

Jane realized what was about to transpire and went to find William Lacy. He was the constable and would hopefully, be able to calm the crowd. Jane ran holding her dress high and trying to keep from slipping in the mud.

"Not Roy, or please why does it have to be Roy." She felt she was screaming yet no sound came from her lips.

Jane clutched her heart; pain pulsating through her body as she gasped for air. She was barely coherent when she finally found the Lacys.

"Help, she screamed, please William, come quick there has been an accident and the people are blaming David Adams."

Elizabeth tried to console her but it was no use. Jane was beyond calming. Yet, she knew she had to calm down for Jessica's sake.

"I must find Jessica. I must give her a message from Dave." Jane was almost delirious as she ran to where she had last seen Jessica.

When Jane got there, some of Jessica's friends were already there comforting her and others were there screaming that her husband killed Roy. That accusation and the fact that Roy was dead were almost more than Jane could bear. Yet, she had to think of what Jessica was going through. She needed to be there for her. Jessica was sobbing uncontrollably. Parson Jones looked haggard as Jane approached him.

"I knew something like this would happen. It was only a matter of time. Indian and White's don't mix." Parson Jones spat out, although, Jane could see he was only thinking of what Jessica was going through.

Jane grabbed the Parson's arm and said, "Dave wouldn't have brought the body back, had he caused Roy's accident in any way. Of all people, he would have been the last to carry a dead white boy back to a crowd of people still scared from the war."

Parson Jones looked Jane in the eye and said, "I know that. However, tell this to these people. They're still looking for revenge, for crying out loud. Now I have to worry about my daughter and a half-breed child."

Parson Jones walked over to his daughter, hunched over shaking his head as he went. He picked up the child and put his arm around his daughter. She pushed him away and told him she would be okay. Jessica took her child from his arms and told him she would be going home.

Jane went over to her and told her she could stay with her if she wanted until this thing was resolved.

"Thanks Jane, you are a real friend, and knowing I can count on you is more help than you know."

Jessica held her little boy close to her to try and ease her pain. She had known the art of survival before and prayed to get through this crisis, for her baby's sake. She knew the best thing for her and her child was to go home. They lived about thirty miles northwest of Duanesburg, and though it would be a hard trip to make on her own, she decided she must do it.

"Jessica, Dave wanted me to tell you he would be back and he loved you." Jane whispered into Jessica's ear as she comforted her before she left.

Jane tried to convince Jessica she should stay with her a while. However, Jessica was firm with her decision.

"I must go home, Jane. If Dave were to come back, I need to be there. I only hope his name is cleared first. Dave can't be separated from us very long. I appreciate the offer and will remember it if I need a place to go and someone I can count on."

Jane couldn't let Jessica go without an escort, so she went once more to William Lacy.

"Would you find someone to escort Jessica and her baby home? She is determined to go, and even though she is strong and can drive a team and wagon, I think she could use some help at this time."

Justin and Josh Mathews were standing with William. Justin piped up,

"I'll go with her." Justin and Roy were close friends, and he also knew it had to be an accident. Josh Mathews agreed to ride with him.

Jane watched as the boys guided the team out of town. It was the first moment Jane had time to really digest what had happened and acknowledge the deep hurt she was feeling. She clutched her arms to her stomach and moaned, "Where are you, Thomas?" Jane knew that he couldn't be here until evening, but that didn't stop the question. If there was a time when she needed someone to lean on, it was now.

"Please, Thomas, I need you so."

Jane couldn't help but plead for him. She was sobbing and voicing the words out loud. Empty words, for they were not answered. It seemed that she waited forever before the comfort she needed was there.

Jane was in her room in the back when she heard the wagon pull up beside the school. She was devastated and must have looked it from the pity she saw in Thomas' eyes.

Jane rushed into his arms and soaked up his strength. Thomas held her tightly until she regained her composure.

"Oh, Thomas, I am so glad you are here. I felt so alone."

"Where are Hugh and Elizabeth?" Jane could hear the pain in his voice.

"They went to Albany this year. Hugh's family was getting together and they decided it is time they went there."

"I am so sorry, Jane. I should have been here. I should have taken the day off."

"You can't help it, Thomas, and this horrible thing should have never happened. The ground was wet from all the rain they had the week before. Roy's horse slipped in a big mud hole going full gallop. Roy had made the same run everyday this week. He wanted so much to win this race. How long can you stay Thomas?" Jane's face was pressed into Thomas's chest.

"I was supposed to be back at work the day after tomorrow; however, now I will stay until after the funeral. I couldn't leave you right now." Thomas wished he could do more to ease Jane's pain.

The funeral was the next day. The sun was shinning brightly, although the whole town was gray with sadness. It seemed that everyone for miles around came for the funeral. There were hushed voices of gossip here and there. Most people, however, were considerate and showed their respect by being silent.

That was the way it was for the rest of the day. This small part of the world was somber. Nobody said anything because they were afraid of the turmoil it would cause.

Thomas stayed with Jane the rest of the day. They spoke very little, and when they did it was small bits of conversation to see how each other were doing.

Thomas left at noon the next day. Jane watched until she could no longer see a glimpse of him. She could feel her heart leave with him. The spot where her heart should be was empty. She didn't know when she would see him again. Thomas said he might try to come home over the holidays. However, not to count on it because he needed to work as much as possible and also the weather might not permit it.

CHAPTER XVII

Surprise Visit

Almost six months went by. Carrying on without Roy had been difficult. However, Jane decided it was time they all cheered up. She thought it would be nice to have some kind of party. The children decided it would be fun to invite all the parents to the school on the last day before Christmas break. Jane and her students were excited as they planned what they would do for entertainment. As they talked there hands were busy making paper decorations and popcorn balls.

The next morning Josh came to school with a tree. It was kind of sparse; looking like it was missing half its branches and the ones it did have bent over almost to the floor; especially when they put on any decoration with any weight, like popcorn balls. However, the chidren made a lot of decorations and by the time they had put them on the tree and covered up a few of the bare spots, it looked just fine. That evening was the night of the party so Jane decided to let the children make taffy. They were busy most of the day. She let them leave an hour early so they could help their folks with the chores and supper before the party.

It seemed no time before the parents and kids began to file in. The last to arrive were the Lacys. They lived the farthest from town and had a lot of chores to do before they could leave. The large family was entering the room when Jane's heart stopped beating for a second. Thomas was suddenly there a head taller than the children. His eyes beamed as he saw the surprised look on Jane's face.

"Hi, Thomas, I can't believe you're here! Do you not have school this week?"

"No, they decided to give us a break." Thomas was still holding Jane's gaze. "Also, I told them I had to see you one more time before the snow was to deep and hard to travel."

"I can't believe how little snow we have had and it is almost Christmas. This is such a surprise. I didn't think I would see you until summer." Jane held out her hand in greeting.

His touch was so gentle, sending warmth and comfort throughout her body. Jane quickly pulled her hand from his grasp and turned to greet her guests. The children were already organized and anxious to start the program.

They started off with first one song and then another, encouraging their parents to chime in. After the children were through singing, they put on a little skit. After that they were more than ready for refreshments. Jane's donations were cookies, apple cider and coffee. Then her students passed out taffy and popcorn balls to everyone. Next to everyone's surprise, Andrew Herks got up and passed around bags with peanuts and hard candy in them.

By the time everyone was through visiting it was getting late. Jane was glad when the last person left. She was impatient to have Thomas to herself. Thomas stayed for about an hour longer to visit. He told Jane he would be back the next morning and hoped to spend most of the day with her before he had to start back.

The next day Thomas was there early. Jane made him breakfast. It being such a nice day for that time of year, Thomas and Jane decided to go on a drive. They went the route passed the cemetery, leading opposite of town. They wanted to be alone. About a mile up the road there was the clearing where Jane had spent a lot of time. It was high enough up that you could see for miles, looking every direction except one where the woods came up to the edge of the field.

It was so beautiful; the woods frozen white with frost that blended in with a skiff of snow on the ground. It was still early enough that it hadn't melted off. The sun was creeping higher in the sky and they could see that it wouldn't be long before the ice on the trees would be melted and the ground bare once again. However for now the trees and the ground were glistening, almost putting them into a trance.

"Isn't it beautiful, Thomas?"

"It is breathtaking, Jane."

They sat there taking in the wonder of the season. In fact, they sat there, Thomas' arm around her, until all the ice melted from the trees.

CHAPTER XVIII

No Turning Back

Jane felt lonely. Thomas was on his way back to Albany. It had been a wonderful couple of days. However, the silence with everyone being gone was worse than ever for Jane. She decided to read one of the letters that Jessica's father brought to her last week. Parson Jones would come through town every couple of months on his way to Ablany, where he picked up supplies to take back to the small trading post he had put up near where his daughter and Dave now lived.

Jane was glad to know that Jessica was happy and safe with the ones who loved her most. Dave didn't think Jessica would ever become accustomed to the Indians' way of life. However, because they were forced to move closer to his family, Jessica was able to see that the natives were loving, wonderful people. They had built a cabin on the outskirts of the Indian village and Jessica's father built a trading post about a mile from their cabin. Jessica developed a close relationship with Dave's sister. She seemed to have adjusted to this life and was only too happy that her son would have the best of both worlds. Jane continued reading, trying to block out some of the sadness she was having knowing she would not see Jessica as often, and also wouldn't be seeing Thomas until spring. Jane finished reading and was about to blow out the lamp when she heard knocking at her back door. This startled her because no one ever used that door.

"Who would be calling this late at night?" She thought. Jane never had company at night. She cautiously went to the door.

"Who's there?"

"It's me, Billy."

Jane opened the door to the familiar voice.

"How are you, Billy? What do you want at this hour?"

Unexpectedly, Billy pushed the door open.

"I know you love me, and I want to be with you." He grabbed for her.

"What are you doing?" Jane tried to break away.

His voice was strange, unlike Billy's. It was distorted and that of a mad man. He tightened his grip, pushing her backward toward the bed.

"Let go of me," Jane screamed.

Jane was suddenly fighting for her life. She never thought she could have so much fear.

Billy hung on like a vice. Jane tried to squirm away. It was no good. If only she could get to the other side of the bed. She would be able to reach the gun that was leaning against the wall beside the dresser. Billy swung her unto the bed. He held her down and wrestled her until Jane had no strength left. Then the unthinkable happened. Jane was weak from fighting and finally lay limp. Billy finished, turned over and sat on the edge of the bed toward the door. Jane's innate instinct took control. She found renewed strength and felt the power in her come alive. She rolled over and off the bed beside the bureau and grabbed the gun. Getting to her knees, she leaned the gun on the bed doing it all that in one fast continuing movement. Billy was heading for the door. Jane yelled for him to stop. Billy turned, the gun blasted. Blood and flesh spurted unto the door behind Billy. Jane stood and stared at what she just done. She was numb, and in a different world. She saw Billy's body on the floor, a pool of blood slowly forming a puddle. Then Jane's instinct took over again and she pulled the blood tainted blanket from the bed and rolled Billy onto it.

Then she grabbed her hair with her blood tainted hands and cryed out. "What have I done? What have I done? What have I done?"

Jane saw her world crumbling. She could never let anyone know. She felt such shame and guilt and a total change came over her. Jane was a different person. It was a stranger that gathered up the strength to do what needed to be done. Jane remembered old Granny Jessup being buried two days before. The dirt would still be loose enough for her to dig. Jane would get the shovel and bury Billy there, over the top of Granny Jessup. She grabbed the corners of the blanket and tugged as hard as she could; surprisingly, it pulled easily, at least until she got to the deep grass. Even though, it wasn't all that far to the tree line between the school and the cemetery, it seemed to take an eternity. The body wanted to slip off the blanket, and she would roll him back on again. Jane tried to slide him without the blanket but couldn't get a good grip on his arms as her hands weren't big enough. She finished dragging the body to the side of Granny Jessup's grave and ran for the spade that was leaning against the outhouse a few feet from the school.

In an utmost frenzy Jane began to shovel the fresh dug dirt from the top of Granny's grave. Scoop after scoop, then stumbled into the hole and used her hands. It seemed that she couldn't stop. After she dug the hole deep enough so that no animal would be able to exhume the body, she rolled Billy, blanket and all, into the shallow grave, then tossed furiously shovel after shovel of dirt trying to put out of sight not only Billy, but the horror of that night.

But the horror was just beginning. Jane walked as though in a trance back to the school and in through the door to her room. She had to sidestep the pool of blood, spread even futher from dragging Billy's body though it. Then she took off her blood soiled clothing and tried in vain to wipe the blood from the floor. She went into the school room and shoved the clothing into the fireplace. Then went back to finish cleaning up the rest of the blood spattered room. Jane went to the well outside the school and drew up bucket after bucket of water and poured it into a wooden tub that was in the school room by the fireplace. She proceeded to draw more water taking it into her room and tossing it over the blood stained floor and began to sweep the bloody liquid out the door. She then again, got another bucket and threw the water on the door itself in hopes of cleaning off the blood spatters. After she was finished with that she climbed into the tub of icy cold water and scrubbed until she was raw.

Jane was shivering uncontrollably as she took a quick look around making sure everything was clean. She noticed that where the blood was on the floor and door had darkened the wood. She took the rug that was in the entry to the schoolroom, and put it over the blood spot by her back door. Next she found a blanket and hung it over the door after she closed and locked it. All this she did without thinking to put on any clothing. Then Jane looked around and found her robe. She went to the rocking chair in the corner of the room and sat staring straight ahead seeing nothing. Rocking, Rocking. Tears silently rolled down her cheeks.

Jane was startled by a horse neighing as someone was securing it to the hitching post. She was jolted back to sanity. She looked into the mirror. Seeing the scratches and bruises on her face brought back instant memories of last nights horror and the nightmare once again revived. Her arms were bruised as was the rest of her body. She remembered putting the blood drench nightgown in the fireplace. She didn't know if it was entirely burned.

"It must smell as though someone gutted a deer in here," she thought.

Jane regained her senses, and covering her head, she opened the door a crack to see who was there. It was Reverend Bogert. After telling him she had the flu, and would be ok. She went back to the rocking chair; thinking of nothing but the squeak of the rockers as they rolled back and forth, back and forth.

Jane stayed in that same rocker, except to go to the toilet, and being disturbed by the Reverend out of concern for her health, for three days. She had no desire to eat. She had no desire to think. She had no desire to even dress herself. However, there was a sense in the back of her mind that told her she must to go on. The third day she quit rocking and began to work. After which she cleaned herself and every piece of furniture, clothing, and dish in her small dwelling. When she was finished and the flannel bedding was dry on the line, Jane brought them in and made the bed. She then spread the old horsehair rug; Hugh had given her, over the bed for added warmth. Jane's only quilt was buried with old granny Jessup.

Jane then went into the school room and started to clean in there. She worked the night away and into the morning scrubbing desks, washing walls, and sweeping, and finished by mopping the floor on her hands and knees. Jane had lost count of what day it was. She assumed it was still Christmas break. It still hadn't snowed much. However, it did snow about an inch the night after the incident. Jane thought, this was good, because it covered any trace of Billy's body being drug to the cemetery.

As Jane was standing in the doorway of the school looking around at the fresh snow, she saw Justin riding toward the school. As usual, he was the first one there after the break.

"I hear you have been ill, Miss Jane. Will there be school today?" He hollered from outside.

Jane hesitated before she stuck her head out the door to answer him.

"Yes, there will be, Justin. Would you like to spread the word?"

Justin was only too eager to ride off like Paul Revere and spread the word.

It didn't take him long before he was back and asking her if there was anything else she wanted him to do.

"Would you like to draw a bucket of drinking water?"

Jane remembered that she forgot to fill the bucket and the kids always seemed to be in need of a drink of water.

Justin brought the water in and set the bucket on the stand by the wash basin, grabbing the dipper hanging on a peg above the bucket, he took a long drink of cold water. Next he turned and looked around the room.

"What's different in here Miss Jane?"

"I changed the tables around so they face the blackboard. I think we'll start changing the room around once a week so we can all start the week off fresh and new."

The children started to file into the room.

"Where do we sit?" chimed in a melody of voices.

Jane laughed for the first time in days.

"We will draw names to see where each of you will sit."

The kids were excited for the change in routine and were happy to be back in school.

School went on as usual. Jane went on as usual. There seemed to be a cloud wherever she went. She laughed, she talked, she taught. However, it seemed that her heart and soul were missing. There was a black hole in the center of her being and it seemed there was nothing that could ever put the light back.

If only she had someone to talk too. Maybe there wouldn't be so much gloom. Maybe they would hold her and say everything would be okay. If only she could see Thomas, she would lay her head on his chest and let all thoughts float away and tell him what happened and hope he would understand the wrong she did; murder.

If anyone were to know that she committed murder she would be hung. She must remain quiet. Never tell a soul. She knew that God knows, and that she was already condemned to hell. However, God was just; he would know the whole picture and see that she wasn't herself when she pulled the trigger. She shook her head to rid the thoughts from her mind. If only she could forget.

Jane shook her head again as Betsy was trying to get her attention saying her name over and over.

"What's the mater, Miss Jane? Miss Jane, Miss Jane!"

Betsy was a blur before her. She needed to regain her composure.

"I'm sorry, Betsy. Do you want something?"

"No, Miss Jane, you were in a daze and it is time for recess."

"The time sure went by fast this morning." Once again Jane tried to compose herself.

"You seem to be in another world Miss Jane. Is something bothering you?" Betsy showed concern for her.

"I haven't been feeling well and was sick during Christmas break."

"Maybe you're not quite well yet." Betsy's sounded worried.

"I'm all right, Betsy. I didn't sleep well last night with thinking about how to start the school day. I just need to calm down a little. You go outside and take a break and stop worrying about me."

Jane thought Betsy worried too much about people's feelings and felt she would make a good doctor. Like her brother William.

Jane watched as Betsy turned toward the door with a worried look on her face. Once Betsy was outside, Jane saw her take a deep breath of fresh air and walk off. Betsy no sooner started her walk when she had three little girls tagging along.

Jane went back to her room, covered her face with her hands and began to weep softly. After a few minutes she went to the wash basin and splashed cold water on her face. Her eyes were bloodshot and swollen. Her face was blotched red. She looked and felt a mess. She didn't know what she was going to do. How was she going to get beyond this awful feeling? She went to the rocker, tired and exhausted from the breakdown. She let the children have an extra fifteen minutes while she composed herself and regained some strength.

She didn't want to face the children in this condition, but knew she had to. Back in the classroom, Jane made it throught the day as though she had a weight on her sole.

Jane didn't know how she would be able to mask what had happened. She didn't know how she made it through that first week. It was all such a blur.

Jane was holding two letters that she had received from Thomas. One came a week ago and one today. She felt it time to read them and send him some kind of answer. He sounded very concerned about her. She didn't know how to tell him she didn't want to be with him any more. With a heavy heart and as tears ran down her cheeks she began to write.

Dear Thomas,

This will be the last letter you will receive from me.
Things have changed for me. My feelings have changed for
you. I feel I owe it to you to tell you now so you can carry
on with your life. I'll cherish the times we have had together.
You are a nice and caring person. I am sure you will be able
to find someone more worthy of you than I am. My life will
be here with the children.

Yours Truly, Jane

The days that followed were involuntary. Jane continued her everyday
tasks in a trance. The children noticed the change and tried to get her to
open up.

"Miss Jane, can I ask you a question?" Jane brought herself to the
presant and tried to stay focused on Mehtilda's question.

"Of course, Mehtilda, what is it you need to know."

"We all want to know what is wrong with you. You seem so far away.
Did something happen between you and Thomas? Mother said you are
no longer seeing him."

The questions were more than Jane could deal with at once. She didn't
realize just how far she was from reality.

Jane told the children they could take a break, and barely made it
to her room before she broke down. "You have got to get control, she
thought to herself. This is enough with self pity."

Jane finally regained composure and decided then and there that she
needed to get a grip on her emotions and do her job.

When she rang the bell for the children to come in, she stayed at the
door and smiled and greeted each child as they entered.

After everyone was in their places, Jane proceeded to answer the
questions that were asked her before recess.

"Class, I am sorry I haven't been myself lately. Yes Mahtilda, Thomas
and I are no longer together. It has been hard to accept. However, starting
right now I will try to be more attentive. I hope this answers all your
questions of why I've been so distant."

After Jane was finished confessing, what hopefully, explained her actions of the last few days, the children one by one expressed their consideration.

Jane felt relieved after making this partial confession and suddenly realized how much better it would be if she had someone to confide in. At that moment Jane had a strong yearning for her real mother. She felt this would be the one person in the world that she would be able to tell.

Jane's heart ached for her mother. Then she remembered the promise she had made herself a few minutes before. Jane brought her mind back to the present and made sure to keep it there until the children were gone.

She managed to put on a false image when she taught during the day, but the rest of the time she spent in anguish.

CHAPTER XIX

The Sun Shines another Day

It was about two month's before Jane began to feel the horror slide behind. She had worked endlessly with an everlasting energy until falling exhausted onto her bed; although, she still had fitful nights with visions of horror. The dreams a mixture of screaming and never-ending darkness that would end with Billy's face, at which time Jane woke in a sweat and found the screaming to be coming from her. It had been days before she slept the night without being awakened by her own screams.

One morning while getting out of bed Jane began to swoon, she caught herself and found she wanted to vomit. She staggered to the pail that was kept in the room to use in case of an emergency. Jane hardly ever needed to go in the night, though she was very glad the pail was handy that morning.

Jane decided to call off school of for a couple of days. She didn't want everyone to get what she had.

Justin arrived early as usual.

"Justin, yelled Jane, could you spread the word there will be no school today. I was sick during the night and need to rest.

"Okay, Miss Jane. Are you going to be okay? Do you need a bucket of water drawn? I'll be glad to do what ever I can to help."

Jane's heart swelled at Justin's concern for her. "I'll be alright, Justin."

A week later Jane was still vomiting and had visions of the way her mother was when she found out she was pregnant with Ellen. Jane's heart sank and she curled up into a ball on the bed as she did when she couldn't accept what she was hearing, and this thought in her mind was one thing Jane hadn't counted on. She was in so much denial and shock she didn't think of the consequences of being raped.

Once again Jane was alone with her thoughts and reality. Once again she was walking a living nightmare. The next few days were a blur to her. She was about to sink back into despair when she had just begun to feel she was pulling out of it. She shook her head to make the thoughts go away. They went only for a while and then would creep back again. Jane couldn't accept a child from being raped. It wasn't fair. She felt she had lost everything when she lost Thomas. She felt it to be impossible to carry on. Now she was going to have to raise a freak. She hated herself for thinking that way. She hated what was happening. She hated her life, and the thought of not wanting to live it would come flooding into her mind.

Jane had always wanted a family. There was the dream of her and Thomas living their lives together and there was always children. Now she was going to have to figure out once more how to cope with her life and the life that was inside her.

She went back to working the day away. It was the only way she could keep the thoughts of what was happening to her out of her mind. First one month went by, then another. Before she knew it May flowers would be in bloom and the early soft green leaves on the trees would become mature leaves. It had been a mild winter. The little bit of snow had melted early and was completely gone in April. Any sign that might have been left of Billy was gone. The early morning sickness had gone away too.

Jane almost felt that there wasn't a baby there at all, except she was getting bigger. She hardly ever thought about being pregnant but when she was wishing it to go away. Then one day while out hanging sheets Jane felt a twinge in her belly. It was a little kick, and Jane's heart gave a twist. It seemed to squeeze the love and want of this little being into her soul. For the first time she forgot where the baby came from. Jane went into her room and sat in the rocking chair. She held the tiny bulge of her tummy and relaxed for the first time in months. With her head against the back of the chair Jane once again began to dream of a future. Only she wasn't alone. She would have a child that would be a part of her and part of her mother. And that was all that mattered.

The next day Jane began sewing. She had some muslin that was left over from making sheets and made some little night gowns and a couple of blankets. That evening she got out her knitting needles and started making a warm sweater for the baby. Jane spent her free time getting ready for this new life that was coming. She felt that after all the weeks of hard physical labor she might have abused her body too much and hoped that it didn't affect the baby.

The baby seemed to be active enough and every time it would kick and squirm, Jane's heart would swell. She made plans to get a message to Hugh and Elizabeth to come and take her home. She decided to let school out the first weekend in May. This way she would be able to hide her pregnancy from the children and other town's people. Jane felt like she was betraying them, yet every time the baby kicked, she felt she had a future; a future that wouldn't include this town or her school children. Jane felt a sudden loss at the thought of leaving. However, she once again dreamed of a family. If only she would have been brave enough to go with Thomas. It would have been so different.

One morning Jane woke to the sun shinning in the window and the beams came across the bulge of her abdomen. In the spot that the sun was brightess she saw movement. Her heart tugged and she took in a gasp of air. She got up and dressed in a cheery yellow dress to match the morning and was humming a tune when Justin got there.

As usual he was the first one to arrive.

"Hello, Miss Jane, he said, you seem so happy today."

"Good morning, Justin, I'm feeling so much better than I have as of late. How are you?"

"Great, is there anything you need done today? Want me to fetch some water from the well?"

"That would be wonderful Justin. The suns so nice and bright there probably won't be any need to build a fire to take off the chill. What do you think?"

"I think it feels fine," he said as he headed out the door with the bucket.

Before long the children began to file in one by one. Although, with the Lacy family it was more like two by two. Jane wondered if the other children noticed the change in her.

As the weeks went by her new found happiness blossomed as did the color in her cheeks. One day Jane told the children that she would be excusing them for early break because Hugh and Elizabeth needed her at home. The children cheered with excitement. Jane smiled as she felt the life inside her stir.

"It will be ok, little one." She thought

Jane was now in her fifth month and the bulge in her stomach was beginning to show. She had got word back from Hugh and Elizabeth. They would be coming to Duanesburg in a couple of weeks. Jane could hardly wait to see them and hoped they would welcome the news better than she did.

It was only a few more days before Hugh and Elizabeth would be there and Jane was busy cleaning and getting ready for them in her usual fast work mode. She had dismissed school the day before and was washing clothes and packing. She took a load of sheets out to hang on the clothsline. She was humming to herself when she bent to pick up a sheet to throw over the line, the way she usually did. Without warning she dropped to her knees in sheer pain. Jane could hardly get up and make it to her room. She felt hot liquid running down her legs. She had bit a hole through her bottom lip to keep from screaming. She barely made it through the door to her room when she fell faint over the bed. Jane was fadding in and out of darkness when she tried to force herself to gather her wits and strength for the inevitable.

Jane doesn't know how she made it through those agonizing moments. Darkness came and went, came and went.

Jane finally came to and discovered herself saturated in blood. She grimaced with another sharp pain. She thought she wasn't only loosing the baby she was losing her life as well. She said a silent prayer for both of them. God answered only one. The tiny little baby girl was born into a world she would never see. As soon as Jane gathered enough strength she reached into her sewing basket and took out a tiny blanket. Then she dumped the sewing things onto the floor, covered her precious little Jenny in one of the blankets she had made and held the baby to her chest until almost dawn. Then wrapping the blanket snuggly around her, Jane gently put her into the sewing basket and once more in the early hours walked to the cemetery carrying her shovel and the basket. Jane walked up a little hill to the far side of the cemetery and there beside an oak tree, dug once again another hole, and once again buried a part of her never to be revealed to another living soul.

CHAPTER XX

When Memories Pause

The next couple of days were beautiful, but, Jane didn't notice. It was gray to her. She was hardly aware of her surroundings at all. It was as though her mind had paused in time. The days went by and she hardly knew it. She never remembered eating. She didn't remember sleeping. She didn't remember going to the toilet. She didn't remember cleaning up the blood stained bedding, but she had. In the back of her mind she knew that Hugh and Elizabeth were coming and that she wanted everything normal. When she was finished, she went to the rocker to wait for Hugh and Elizabeth's arrival.

"Hello!" Jane could faintly hear Hugh as he called her name. "Jane! We're here!"

Hugh entered the school room and made his way to the back. After knocking lightly he and Elizabeth entered Jane's room. It was dark and dreary. The curtains were closed. It was chilly and Jane was sitting so still Hugh instantly knew something wasn't right.

"Jane! Are you ok?" Jane heard the concern in Hugh's voice.

She tried to rise and greet them. In fact, she thought she was saying something, but it seemed they weren't hearing.

"Jane! Jane! Wake up," Yelled Hugh as he shook her.

Hugh shuddered when he saw the blank look in Jane's eyes.

"Something is wrong, Elizabeth. She isn't responding. She has a fever. I had better go for the doctor."

Elizabeth brought a cool cloth to put on Jane's forehead. She stirred but was still unresponsive. The doctor was delivering a baby out in the country and wouldn't be available for several of days.

Hugh and Elizabeth spent two days feeding Jane, trying to nurse her back to health. The fever finally went. It seemed something terrible must have happened to have caused such mental distress. Jane couldn't tell them what caused it. She couldn't seem to speak. She couldn't seem to do anything. Hugh and Elizabeth believed it was because of the loss of one of her pupils. They were both aware of how much Roy meant to Jane, yet thought her strong enough to cope.

Hugh and Elizabeth made a comfortable bed for Jane in the back of the wagon and cared for her on the trip back to the cabin. Jane wouldn't remember the trip at all.

Jane was suddenly jerked awake with the realization that she does remember all. She remembered why Thomas hadn't been to see her and why she wanted to stay void of all memory. Jane sat up on the edge of her bed choking back uncontrollable sobs. She ran to the door to escape her thoughts. She ran to the outhouse still choking and began to heave and choke until she was so weak she felt faint. Jane regained control and went back out into the cool morning air. She decided to take a walk before going back to the house. She didn't want anyone seeing her like this. She had caused enough pain for this family.

Jane did everything in her power to regain her composure. She owed this much to Hugh and Elizabeth. They didn't need to see her in such distress, not after they had cared for her for so long.

"What have I put my family through?" Jane thought.

It's been a week since Jane's memory came back and she woke feeling better than ever. She knew it was time for her to take hold of her life and carry on. She went into the front room stoked the fireplace and got ready to fix her beloved family breakfast.

She heard them stirring in the bedrooms as they were getting ready for the day. They were surprised when they saw Jane was already up and had started breakfast.

"Good morning to my beautiful family."

"Good morning, Jane," they all chimed in.

"How do you want your eggs?" Jane was putting fresh biscuits on the table as she spoke.

After she took their orders they started to speak at once. It was just like old times again. And it was so homey and comfortable. Jane wished she could stay there forever and not have to worry about any of the hardships of life. But she knew it was time to start thinking of her future. Her eyes swelled with tears as she answered the steady stream of questions coming from her family.

CHAPTER XXI

Road to Recovery

It had been several weeks since things started clearing in Jane's mind. The pictures flooded in more and more every day and at times she felt as though she wouldn't be able to handle it all. Her mind wanted to pause again and she had to force herself to keep her memory intact. She felt as though she would suffocate on the past. It was a struggle to stay sane. However, Jane knew she would have to keep busy or she would slip back into the void she was in. That was something she would prevent no matter what.

Just when Jane was becoming anxious to start a new life, Elizabeth got a letter from Hugh Jr. He and his wife lived in Delhi, a small town about a hundred miles south of there. Hugh Jr. wrote to tell them sad news. His wife Janet was suffering an unknown illness. She was fading fast and he wondered if Elizabeth could come and help out until his wife got back on her feet.

Jane saw the weariness in her mothers face as she read the letter out loud to them. Jane immediately spoke up and said she would go to be with Janet. Hugh gave her a thankful look.

"Are you sure you are up to this, Jane?" Elizabeth sounded concerned for her.

Jane put her arms around Elizabeth.

"Mother, you have done so much for me that I will never be able to repay you. Please allow me to do this small thing. I haven't seen Hugh Jr. for so long and I don't even know Janet. This will be a way for me to become reunited with Hugh Jr. and repay some of the care that has been given me."

"I hope you aren't rushing into something that would cause you a lot of stress." Elizabeth was still hesitant over the step Jane was taking.

However, Jane convinced Elizabeth that she would be fine. Jane sent a message to Hugh Jr. that she would be coming instead of Elizabeth. Jane went on to say how sorry Elizabeth was, but she had been a little under the weather and needed to rebuild her health. It would be a couple of weeks before Hugh would be free, because Ellen needed to get back to Albany before the new school year and Hugh would be taking her there first.

This left a few days for Elizabeth and Jane to spend some time together. Jane had never felt so close to Elizabeth. She always loved and respected her, but now there was a closeness that wasn't present before. Jane couldn't show Elizabeth enough how much she appreciated what she had done for her.

"I'm sure going to miss you when I go to Delhi, mother."

"I am so glad you are coming along so well, Jane. You are getting better and that's what's important to me. I don't know what I would have done had you not come out of this ordeal. We were so afraid that we would have to send you away. I wouldn't have been able to forgive myself if we would have had to do that."

"Mother, your love and understanding was the best medicine for me. Had you and Hugh not given the care you did before Ellen came, I probably would not have been alive. Ellen told me how you and Hugh took turns coaxing me to eat and took care of me as though I was a child. And in doing this you have put your health at risk."

"I'm afraid my age is the main cause if my problems."

Elizabeth and Jane were working on a quilt for her to take with when she left there. Jane flinched as she thought of her old quilt, buried with old granny Jessup. Elizabeth had never asked Jane what had happened to her's and Jane had never mentioned it being gone, either. Sometimes when Elizabeth would look at her, Jane thought Elizabeth knew that something horrible had happened. Her eyes seemed so sad and far away. It made Jane wonder how many women had secrets like her. Secrets that were buried into their consciousness only for them to ever see, and she wondered how many of these women have shut off their memories even to themselves; memories that were paused in time, never to awaken.

"Jane, you seem so far away," said Elizabeth.

Jane brought her mind back to the present, shaking her head ridding it of the uncomfortable thoughts.

"I'm wondering how much Hugh Jr. has changed since he left home. I can't believe it's been at least five years since I last saw him, and to think that I have never met his wife. Is she nice, Mother?"

"Hugh couldn't have found anyone better than Janet. I hope she snaps out of this illness. I don't know what Hugh Jr. will do without her."

"Do the doctors know what the problem is?"

"They are unsure. They have seen it before, but haven't determined what it is. They say it is a grave situation though. I fear she will not be with us much longer."

"Does Hugh Jr. know this?"

"Yes, the doctors have told him so, but he is in denial."

Jane never realized Janet was that bad off. She wondered if she would be able to cope with this new endeavor she was about to take.

"Are you going to be all right, Jane? Elizabeth noticed Jane's silence and concern was in her voice.

Jane didn't know if she would be or not, however didn't say that to Elizabeth.

"I think so." She hoped her reply wasn't too weak.

"If you need me, Jane, you let us know."

"I will, mother."

Elizabeth, even though cheerful enough, seemed so thin and frail. Jane felt she had gone through more than she would ever know, taking care of her these last couple of months. Hugh had mentioned to Jane the other day that he thought that this winter would be the last one they would spend there in the country. Elizabeth's brother lived in New York City and they talked about moving near him. The doctors would be close if they needed them and there wouldn't be all the hard physical labor that was on the farm.

"What does father feel about leaving the farm, mother?"

"I'm sure he will miss the wide open spaces. However, he won't miss having to get up in the middle of the night to deliver a calf. We'll both miss the thrill of a new life being brought into the world, though."

"What will you do with the farm?"

"Hugh plans to sell out so we can buy a small place in the city."

"Let me know when you have the sale because I want to be here for it."

"I'm not sure if it will be this spring or the next. We want to stay as long as our bodies let us."

"How are you feeling, mother? You look so tired. I hope I didn't cause this."

"I've been feeling tired and run down for a couple of years, Jane. As I told you before, I'm not getting any younger.

"If you need me to stay and help you, I will. Lord knows I owe it to you."

"You don't owe me anything, Jane. I'm your mother and I love you and did what any mother does for her children."

Jane's heart swelled with love for this woman. She had gone beyond the call of duty. Jane would always remember that. A picture of her real mother flooded her mind. "Mom you are the one I shall always cherish, but Elizabeth has been a true mother to me and I love her dearly for it." Jane felt a small stab of guilt, and then looked up at Elizabeth with heartfelt emotion.

"The same goes for you, mother. If you need me, I'll be here."

Jane would always treasure the time they spent together. It brought them closer than they had ever been before. They had done everything together. Watered and fed the animals, sewed and the other household chores. They stayed in each other's shadow the whole week Hugh was gone. In fact, the week had gone by too fast.

It was late in the evening when Hugh came driving the steeds up to the barn. Jane and Elizabeth went out to greet him.

"Good evening," Jane yelled as she ran toward the barn. Elizabeth was in close pursuit. Jane noticed she was very much out of breath by the time she caught up.

"Are you ok, Mother?"

Jane had to hold her up for a minute while she gulped in air.

"I'm fine, Jane. I'm a little winded, that's all."

Jane and Elizabeth had everything ready to go. However, Hugh needed a couple of days to rest up, and he needed to find someone to look after the farm while they were gone.

Hugh had found a sixteen year old neighbor boy to come and tend the farm while they were gone. Hugh and Elizabeth wanted to spend a few days with thier son. They hadn't seen him in over a year.

Two days later they were loaded and on their way south; Jane was once again, heading off to another opportunity. She shuddered with excitement and fear of the unknown. She felt as though the days ahead would be good ones.

It was the first of August, the day was bright and there's a feel of the coming fall in the morning air. That time Jane didn't have Hugh stop the wagon so she could have one last look. She looked straight into her future.

She was certain that she would never stay at the place of her childhood again.

The trip to Delhi was full of ups and downs, not because they ran into trouble but because there were so many hills to go over. The country looked so stunning when looking down from the hills onto the rolling tops of the black hardwood stands.

They had spent the time to really get to know each other again. Jane knew it would be hard to leave her folks behind this time. The only plus in the situation was that Delhi was closer to New York City than the farm, if Hugh and Elizabeth did indeed move there.

About a half day into the trip south they came upon an area that seemed familiar to Jane. There was a narrow roadway leading through a stand of spruce trees. Jane yelled for Hugh to stop the horses. Hugh did so and turned to Jane. "Jane, do you remember this place?"

"It really looks familiar." Jane began to feel fear as her mind took her way back to a place that she hadn't seen for many years. There were houses built close together around a familiar clearing. None of them looked familiar. She did recognize where one of her close friends once lived. There was the same huge oak tree that had a swing, however, Jane knew it wasn't the same one that she had swung on.

They must have rebuilt in the same place where Jane's family and the Dutch community used to be.

"Father, will you take that road please?"

"Are you sure you're ready for this, Jane"

"I have to face this one last thing." 'Hugh turned the horses onto the road. The farther they went down the road the more breathless Jane felt. Just like that the road came to a small clearing. There was a small log cabin set back against an outline of the forest. Jane had Hugh stop the horses.

She then climbed down from the wagon and slowly walked up to the door. The door was ajar. Jane looked into a very familiar place. Everything was the same. The fireplace, the hearth that Jane sat on when she read, and the table, were all the same. A lady came to the door.

"Can I help you?" Jane didn't hear or see the lady at first. Hugh came up behind Jane. "Miss., this is the cabin of Jane's childhood. Her family, along with several other families was massacred in the 80's. Jane and her sister were found in an old dry well behind the cabin.

"May I come in?" Jane's voice was strained and hard to understand.

"She wants to know if she can come in." Hugh repeated Jane's words.

The lady stepped aside so Jane could enter the cabin. Jane walked straight to the ladder that led to the loft. She grabbed the first rung of the ladder. Her hands began to instantly sweat. However, she made it to the top. There was her book setting on a wooden crate used as a night stand. On the bed was a faded quilt. The one her mother had made. She picked up one corner of the quilt and held it against her cheek. She sat like that for several minutes. Finally Hugh climbed part way up the ladder and told Jane it was time to go.

"This stuff belongs to my Mother." Jane was blunt, almost hostile.

"This is the way we found the cabin many years ago. Nobody ever came back to claim anything. It was the only place that wasn't burned. I think it was sheltered enough by the woods and was overlooked."

Hugh had taken the girls and gone home with them. The other men had gone home too after making sure there were nobody left alive and the bodies given a proper burial. Hugh was just as surprised as Jane to see the cabin untouched.

Elizabeth coaxed Jane down from the loft. Jane still had the book in her hand. "May I keep this book? I'm sorry; I didn't get your name. I'm Jane these are my parents, Hugh and Elizabeth Kruffman." Jane seemed to be recovering from the shock delt her.

"I'm Kathern Baker and this is my husband Bill." Bill was just walking up to the cabin from the barn. "Bill, these are the Kruffman's."

Bill extended his hand. "I've heard the name. Please to meet you."

While Hugh and Bill struck up a conversation, Jane decided to walk around the buildings and refresh her memories. She hadn't gotten very far when she sensed impending doom. She covered her ears. She could smell the smoke, hear the screams. There before her was a familiar area. Jane knew if she were to go though the brush that had gotten thicker and taller over the years, she would find the hole where she and baby Ellen were put.

Hugh and Elizabeth found her standing at the edge of the tangled thicket. Hugh took her by the arm. "I think you have seen enough, Jane. It's time we were on our way."

The three of them road in silence for the next several miles before Jane finely broke the silence "I feel that I have met the last of my demons," she said with a sigh of relief.

"I think you have had to deal with a lot more than you deserve, Jane, said Elizabeth. I wish the road ahead of you to be free of any more sorrow or hardship." However, Elizabeth knew that life didn't work that way. Whatever comes your way must be met head on. Fighting demons throughout life was what made you stronger.

Jane knew she wasn't the only person who had gone through hardships and sorrow. She could see by the way the country side had built up that somebody probably had lived there before. She only hoped these new people didn't have to go through the hardships the ones before them did.

Because there was a scattering of communities that had sprung up over the area around Delhi, it made it a much safer and easier trip than the one to Duanesburg, and they were able to spend a couple of nights at a boarding house.

It was while they were traveling to Delhi that Elizabeth told Jane that Jessica and Dave had come to visit while she was ill. Jane had thought about them often since her memory had returned. She didn't think to check and see if Elizabeth and Hugh had heard from them or not. They lived so far away that Jane thought it would have been hard for them to keep in touch.

"How are Jessica and Dave doing?"

"There are fine, however, they still have to avoid Duanesburg. Some of the people are still insistent that he was the cause of what had happened to Roy." Hugh sounded angry to Jane when he said this. He knew that Dave was incapable of hurting an innocent person.

"Actually, all four of them are doing well. They like it where they are and Jessica is well accepted by Dave's people." Elizabeth eyes beamed as she told Jane about the new baby.

"It's a little girl. She is going to be dark like her brother, except she has blue eyes like her mother. You should see Davy; his hair is long and black. His eyes are like coal and there is always a twinkle in them. He is chubby and it is so cute to watch him running around. He seems to be one with the land. I hope he doesn't have to go through what his father's family has gone through."

"I would think it is time that people learn to get along and understand each other better. I can't believe the government to uproot the Indians again and confine them to an area. They are so use to being free. Now they need to adapt to a whole new way of living. It's not fair." Jane couldn't help but to ramble on. She could only imagine what Dave and Jessica had to go through after Roy's accident. If it weren't for William Lacy keeping control of things, heavens only knows what might have happened.

Elizabeth had told Jane that William Lacy, Thomas' brother, had come to the farm to advise them on her condition.

"He's a doctor now, Jane, and works in an asylmn for the mental insane.

Jane flinched when Elizabeth said insane. Melancholy was a disease that seemed to pass down from family to family. Therefore, Jane was glad that she no longer was with Thomas. She felt the sadness as it penetrated her heart. Jane still had a hard time thinking of Thomas.

Jane never brought up Thomas' name and neither did Elizabeth or Hugh. She was thankful for that. One day maybe Jane would be able to unburden her heart.

They had become quiet and stayed so for several miles each of them in their own thoughts. Jane couldn't rid Thomas' face from her mind. It seemed only yesterday that he had held her in his arms and told her he wanted her to be with him forever. Jane felt the tears well up.

Once again there was silence in the wagon. Dusk was setting in. It was time to find a suitable spot to camp. Hugh had hoped they would have found a place that provided food and a bed. It didn't happen so when they came upon a creek, that had a small clearing where it was obvious that others had camped, they decided it to be the spot.

The evening was perfect. There was a beautiful sunset that you could make out through the black silhouette of the trees. There was a promise of good weather ahead. The camp was sullen to begin with. Then, Jane began to sing. It wasn't long before they were pondering on happy times. They talked until the night life became active and they finally fell into an exhausted sleep.

The next day they headed into the town of Delhi. Hugh Jr. lived on the far side of the village, on a road Jane would become familiar with. Hugh Jr. was waiting on the porch in front of his home. His house was a one story slab home with a porch that extended the width of the house. Hugh Jr. waved and made his way down the steps of the porch. He had reached their wagon and was on hand to help Elizabeth down first. After hugs and more hugs, they turned toward the house. They entered the front door and came into a well kept living room. There was a wood stove in the corner and there was an easy chair and a rocker by the stove. At the far end of the room were a modern cook stove and small table and four chairs. Off the kitchen was a door that led into a bedroom where Janet was resting. After they finally calmed down, Hugh Jr. took them to see Janet. Her illness had confined her to bed.

Janet was beautiful, her long blond hair spred out over her pillow. Her eyes were large and soft blue and they stood out because of the black rings beneath them. She was smiling even though one could tell the misery she was in.

Hugh Jr. introduced Jane, to her. She reached weakly to shake Jane's hand. Her hands were white and cold to the touch.

"I'm sorry my hands are so cold."

"That's all right; it means you have a warm heart."

"It is so good to finally meet you, Janet."

"I'm glad to meet you to, Jane. Hugh Jr. was so excited when he heard you were coming. He said he hasn't seen you since you were kids."

"That is right. Hugh Jr. had stayed in Scotland after the war and then went to work in New York. He was home maybe twice in the last five years and I was gone one of those times." Jane felt she was taking valuable time away from Hugh and Elizabeth.

"Excuse me Janet. We will have lots of time to get to know each other after Hugh and Elizabeth leave."

Jane then left the room to check out the place she would be living. She noticed that there was another bedroom off the kitchen. The bed was made up with fresh linen and Jane wondered if Hugh Jr. had done it or had someone come in to help with the housework. She felt someone behind her and turned to find Hugh Jr. He looked worn out.

"How are you Hugh Jr.?" said Jane.

"I think things will be okay now that you are here Jane. This is your room. I will go and get your things so you can unpack. It is so good to see you."

"I'm glad to be here. Janet seems like a sweet person."

"That she is, Jane."

Hugh brought in Jane's things and she unpacked while her folks visited with Janet.

The next few days were wonderful and they were able to spend every minute catching up on the last five years. Hugh helped his son with the chores and Elizabeth stayed by Janet's side. Janet was feeling quite well during their stay and insisted they include her in everything. The time went quickly.

It was the morning that Hugh and Elizabeth were to leave. Jane had just gotten Janet up and dressed. She could hear the others in the next room. She had made a pot of coffee earlier and could here the clanking of the cups and saucers.

"It sounds like everyone is enjoying their morning coffee." Jane said, as she was putting a comb in Janet's hair to hold it back out of her face.

"Yes, and I think I'm in the mood for a cup myself." Janet sounded in good spirits that morning.

Jane and Janet then walked into the next room. Jane had to grab a hold of Janet to steady her. Though, she did well at making it to the table on her own.

"Good-morning folks," Janet was the first to speak.

"Good-morning to you too," chorused the three at the table.

Jane went about her job of preparing breakfast as the others continued the conversation they had started the day before.

As Jane was setting the plate of eggs on the table, she heard Hugh telling his son that he and Elizabeth would be selling out soon.

"How soon will that be?"

"Most likely it will be this coming summer. Your mother and I haven't been feeling the best these last couple of years. Elizabeth would like to move to New York City so she can be close to her brother. She hasn't seen him in years and would like to be close to her family for a change. I think she would go back to Scotland to be with her parents, if it weren't for you boys being here in America."

"I think she would be better off going to Scotland, Father. The diseases seem to spread easily in New York."

"I know, but they are just as bad in Glasgow." Hugh didn't mention the fact that he also, didn't think being on board ship would be the best thing for his wife.

"I guess you're right, father, and there are some good doctors in New York. When you do this, let me know. I would like to help if I can."

"Thanks son, Hugh had finished eating and waited for the rest to finish, before he suggested they all go outside.

It was a nice morning. They all sat under Janet's favorite oak tree that was on the edge of the yard. Hugh Jr. helped Janet outside so she could be with them. His folks were planning on leaving for home and Janet wanted to be included in seeing Hugh and Elizabeth off. The time went by to fast.

111

Hugh got up and told Elizabeth to stay and visit while he got their bags. They were soon on their way north. It was time they went home. The season was coming to an end, and it was harvest time. If they were to beat the winter, they couldn't spare any more time away from the farm.

CHAPTER XXII

Bittersweet Moments

The stay with Hugh Jr. and Janet proved to be healing for Jane. She came to love Janet. There was always a smile on her face, although often you could see the pain in her eyes. The day by day strength that Janet had always put forth made Jane's problems seem the lesser. The more Janet had to cope, the more Jane's nightmares faded.

August was on their side and the weather was such that Jane could take Janet outdoors everyday. They would sit in the shade of the old oak tree that Janet loved. They spent the time reading books and discussing them. Jane loved to read out loud and Janet seemed to appreciate her doing so.

"What do you want me to read today, Ellen?" Jane had brought several of her books with her so Janet had a change from the books that her husband had acquired while in school and at his grandmother's in Scotland.

"I like the collection of poetry and short stories you have that's written by, Margret Cavendish."

Jane had brought this book back with her when they had left Scotland.

"I love her writtings too." Jane had read for about an hour and thought it was time that Janet went in so she could get some rest. They both would rather have stayed and read on into the day.

Some days Janet had strength enough to walk outside without Jane's help. Other times Hugh Jr. would carry her out to the chair he had built especially for her. Janet would nestle her head into his neck and hang on to him as long as she could before Hugh Jr. put her into the chair. Jane's heart broke a little as she watched because she could feel the care they had for each other. Jane now knew that she would have to be the strong one if the day came when Janet was no longer with them. Hugh Jr. would be lost without his wife. Jane prayed this didn't happen for a long time, even though a sudden feeling of dread waved through her body.

Sometimes, Hugh Jr. would stay and visit with them for a while before he had to attend to his chores. He always updated Janet on how the animals were and would let her know if there was a new calf or a new batch of chicks. Janet loved those times.

"What's new on the farm?" Janet had a smile on her face as she asked her husband for an update.

"The corn is starting to tassel out. It looks like we're going to have an early harvest.

"Good, you shouldn't have to be plowing fields in the cold, this year."

"So far it looks the case, Janet." He said, telling Jane how the year before it had started to rain in September and kept it up until the snow. After visiting together for a few minutes Jane saw that Hugh and his wife were only in tune for each other.

Jane left them and took a stroll around the yard. She stopped at the barn to pet the young stock and talk to old Betsy. Betsy was a beautiful Jersey cow, that every day gave faithfully a gallon bucket of the richest milk. In the morning when Jane would get the milk from the creek where it was kept cool over night, she would skim a good two cups of cream off the top; the first cup being the richest. Jane liked to make Janet a pan of nice creamy vanilla pudding with this. She loved it and could eat pudding and custard where it was hard for her to eat anything else and keep it down.

On the other hand, Hugh Jr. loved to have some of the thick cream over bread with a little sugar. Jane was in trouble if she didn't save him any.

One day about a week after Jane had arrived she asked Hugh Jr. if she could harness up the horse, old Nel, and go out for a drive. He was hesitant at first until she reminded him that she had done this many times before. Dad had taught all of them to harness and drive a team, including Elizabeth.

"Don't worry about me Hugh Jr., I won't be gone long."

"You can be gone as long as you like, Jane. This is your free time, so take advantage of it. Please don't run old Nel to fast. She is getting pretty old. However, I shouldn't have to worry about her running away with you."

"I'll take it easy. I haven't driven a lot lately so I'll start out slow." Jane ordered the horse ahead, and waved at Janet, who was already sitting out under the oak, as she drove by.

This was the first time Jane had been on the road east and this was when she discovered the spot that would comfort and soothe away any tension that built up during the week. The road had several hills before Jane came to one that overlooked a huge valley. There was a small church at the top of the hill. There was a cemetery behind it with several slate markers peeking through the trees. It looked sheltered sitting there amongst the trees in the sanctity of the church.

Jane parked the buggy in the church yard and walked across the road to the shade of an elm tree and took out a book and sandwich from her bag and spent a couple of hours reading and absorbing nature.

When she got back home, she was ready for the task at hand. Janet was already in her room sleeping comfortably so Jane took this time to clean and do any baking that needed to be done. Hugh Jr. usually had the water and wood hauled in and there was water on the fire and hot at all times. This was a luxury that Jane never had in Duanesburg, although, she would never forget how helpful the children were, hauling in the wood and water during the school year.

Jane found she was thinking of the children and the satisfaction she got teaching. She desided that as soon as Hugh Jr. no longer needed her help, she would look for another teaching position.

The days went by and Jane made many trips to the spot on the hill. She had fallen in love with the area. She would sit beneath the elm tree and dream of her future; something that she had given up on a few months ago. After reading several chapters in her book, she would take a short walk, after which, she was ready to head back to the house.

Jane was in the kitchen and a mile away dreaming of what was to come. Hugh Jr. slammed the door as he came into the house. She was about to take a roast from the oven.

"Boy, it sure smells good in here. And I'm starving."

"I'm glad you're hungry, because I've lots for you to eat." Jane's heart was pounding from the interuption.

The cast iron kettle not only had a roast in it, it was also brimming full of potatoes and carrots. Jane had made biscuits earlier and they were already on the table.

While Hugh Jr. was washing up Jane went to see if Janet felt like getting up for supper.

"Janet, would you like to come to the table to eat tonight?"

Janet weakly turned her head toward Jane. Janet looked so frail lying there. Her eyes had such a sunken look.

"I'm not feeling at all well tonight, Jane."

Jane reached for a glass of water from the nightstand and coaxed Janet to take a small sip. That was all she took too. Jane felt she was taking a turn for the worse again. She also feared Janet wasn't going to snap back for an occasional good spell like she had been doing sense Jane's arrival.

"You go ahead and rest, Janet. I will make you some broth and custard. Will this be ok?"

"Thank you Jane, I appreciate all that you are doing for me."

Hugh Jr. was standing in the door-way when Jane turned to go back into the kitchen. She could see the sadness in his eyes. Jane told him Janet wasn't feeling well enough to come out to supper.

Hugh Jr. went over to the bedside, and bent to gently kiss his beloved wife's forehead.

All was silent. The only noises were the clinking of the utensils. Jane decided to leave him with his thoughts. Sometimes that was necessary; when there was nothing to say that made the situation better, silence was the best medicine.

After they finished eating Hugh Jr. got up, grabbed his hat from the peg by the door, and went outside. He walked off toward the corn field. Jane watched as he walked into the distance, until he was out of sight among the tall green corn stalks.

Jane gathered up the dirty dishes, washed and put them away. Then she prepared soup and pudding for Janet. Before bringing the food to her, Jane helped her to the commode. While she waited for Janet she freshened the bedding and laid out something different for her to wear. Then Jane helped her into bed. She had gotten frailer than she was a week ago. Jane propped a couple of pillows behind her head then went to get the pudding. When she came back into the room she saw that Janet's head was hanging limp to her shoulder. She was twitching and saliva was coming from her mouth. Jane put the tray on the dresser and tried to help her.

However, Jane really didn't know what to do. She had heard of seizures, but never seen anyone actually having one. The seizure lasted only a few minutes. Janet's eyes were glazed over. Jane asked if she would be all right while she went for the doctor. Janet nodded her head yes. Jane then went to the barn to hitch the horse to the buggy. She was almost finished when Hugh Jr. came into view.

"Where are you going, Jane?"

"Janet had a seizure so I'm going to get the doctor."

"Is she all right?"

Hugh's face turned instantly pale. He had to hang on to the hitching post to stay standing.

"She is fine right now. I asked her if she wanted the doctor and she nodded yes. I think you should go to her. I'll be right back. Will you be all right?"

Jane was already on the buggy as she spoke to him.

"I'll be fine, but please be quick."

It was only a couple of miles to the doctor's yet it seemed to be a hundred. It was the longest trip Jane ever took. She only hoped the doctor was in when she got there. His house was off the road and up a steep incline. He had steps going up to the door. Jane was out of breath when she got there. Fortunately, he was in.

After giving the doctor the symptoms he gathered his bag and a bottle of some kind of tonic and followed Jane out the door.

The doctor was in the room with Hugh and Janet for what seemed like a long time. Jane could hear them speaking from where she was sitting but couldn't make out the words. Hugh Jr. looked distraught when he and the doctor entered the front room.

After the doctor left, he told Jane the diagnosis. It was as she suspected. Janet was slowly fading away. The doctor left pain medications that would give her temporary relief from her discomfort. He gave her a dose before he left. Janet was sleeping comfortably by the time the doctor had gone. The tonic he gave her was doing its job.

Hugh Jr. turned to Jane and said, "I'm going out for a walk while Janet rests."

"I be right by her side while you're gone."

"Thanks Jane, I don't know what I would do without you."

Jane was sitting in a chair by Janet's bed when she heard the door close in the next room. She knew that Hugh Jr. had left, and never left Janet's side until he came back. At which time, he took her place; a place where he stayed throughout the night.

Janet was looking and feeling much better when Jane brought her breakfast the next morning. She had actually eaten several small bites of bread and was enjoying a cup of tea with lots of cream and sugar. She even had a little color in her face.

Janet seemed to have rebounded. Jane knew that was because of the medicine. It was good to see her that way.

"Do you feel like going outside for an hour or so, Janet? It is so nice out. The leaves are beginning to change color."

"Yes, I must watch the coming in of fall. It's my favorite time of the year." Jane could see the excitement in Janet's eyes.

Jane went to see if Hugh Jr. was finished with his chores so he could carry Janet out to her chair. He seemed elated to do so.

"I'll be happy to do that, Jane. I could sit with her if you want a little time to yourself."

"I might take a ride up to the church. I haven't gone there for a while."

"You go ahead Jane. You need a break. I don't need you to get sick. If you go and get Janet ready I will hitch up the buggy and bring it up to the house for you."

In no time at all, Jane was sailing down the road. The horse was galloping at a fast yet smooth gallop. Jane let her continue at this pace for ten minutes or so, and then remembered Hugh Jr. telling her not to run old Nel too much. She decided to slow down and enjoy the outing. The leaves were turning a soft yellow with mixtures of browns and oranges. The red of the hardwood trees were waiting to burst through and add to the array.

Off in the distance Jane saw the church as she guided old Nel to the top of the hill. She parked the buggy and tied the horse to the hitching post. She had planned to take a walk up the winding trail that continued further up the side of an even steeper incline that was about a mile from where the church was. The trail was a shortcut to a village beyond. Because of the ruggedness of the hill and the danger that lurked in the rough terrain, that hill became known as the Devil's Backbone. Jane decided she would take the trail a ways in and see if it was indeed the devils backbone.

As she crossed the main road to the elm tree where she usually sat, and soaked up the sun and read. Jane looked up from her book and down into the valley that she had come to love so and claimed as her own. To her surprise there was a building being constructed in the lower mid section of the clearing. Jane's heart tugged as she realized the place of her dreams would never be. She turned toward the Devils Backbone and made her way up the hillside sending rocks and dirt cascading down behind.

Jane walked on for about a half hour before she saw why this path received such a name. She turned to go back at that point. The trail was narrow. Jane went as far as she could on a foot path that went along the edge of a deep ravine. It proved to be a much harsher walk than she had thought. However, it felt good to have gone the distance she had.

Jane got back to the church and spent about another hour under the elm tree reading. She could see the horse was getting restless and most likely was in need of a drink. She reluctantly rose and left the area of serenity, and took old Nel to the trough and let her drink. Then, before Jane left, she refilled the troth so there was water for the horses on Sunday.

It was time go to back and start supper. Hugh Jr. was waiting for Jane on the porch. He met her as she turned into the yard and took the horse and buggy to the barn for her.

That became a habit for Jane, for she continued to ride out to the hill until the fall turned into winter. And still did so after the first several frosts. Every time she went out to her favorite spot, she would see another transformation to the farm below. Each time there was a little more done to the house. One time there was a new fenced in area. The next time a few cattle and two work horses. Yet another time there was a man walking behind the horses, so far off in the distance they looked like specks. Jane was happy to see the progression of the farm below. By the end of the season it had materialized before her eyes into a thriving farm. Jane was sure by spring there would be a family added to the scene.

However, once the snow arrived she was hesitant to make the trip alone. This was when she turned to other things to pass the time. Jane started walking the two miles into Delhi and attended some of the church functions. The walk was refreshing. The ladies met in the early afternoon, so she made it home before the sun set. Jane found this to be as relaxing as the ride out to the cabin.

Most of Jane's time was spent taking care of Janet. The winter was hard on her. Jane was happy when the first signs of spring came.

Finally, winter had turned to spring with an array of sunshine that warmed the earth and ignited a rebirth of life. The calves arrived one by one. One of the old nags had given birth to a lovely colt. Jane immediately fell in love with her, a beautiful black filly with a star in the middle of her forehead. Needless to say, Jane named her that, Star. She now occupied some of her time by playing with the colt and teaching her to lead at the same time. It felt so good seeing all the new life around.

The trees were in full bud and about ready to burst forth with a new summer cloak; first the soft tender green, then a burst of luscious mature leaves, giving the feel of embracement. The beginning of spring left an aroma, of new earth with a mixture of wild roses and lilacs, as they came to life. Jane felt, spring was the beginning of the cycle of life, a time to start afresh.

Jane's heart rekindled as she looked around and saw how the earth would start anew year after year. Nature seemed to regenerate and do what it took to survive. Jane knew now that she was a survivor. She only wished Janet could win her battle. It's as though Jane had absorbed the last ounce of Janet's strength, for as Jane got stronger, Janet, got weaker.

The battle Janet fought was nearing an end. They had moved her out into the front room so she would be closer to the heat over winter. Now that the weather was warming up they decided it was time to move her back into the bedroom where she was less apt to be disturbed.

Janet had been fading in and out of a coma for the past month. Her body had withered away over the winter. Yet when she was awake she always put forth a smile and was always the one to tell Hugh Jr. and Jane that it would be okay.

However, it hadn't been okay with Hugh Jr. Jane saw the pain in his eyes as he sat by Janet's bedside. He always had her hand in his. When she was sleeping peacefully Hugh Jr. would bend forward and lay his head on the bed as if praying for her comfort. He didn't leave her side. It had been that way since Janet started fading in and out of consciousness. Every evening after Hugh Jr. finished his work for the day; he would go in and sit with his wife.

"Hugh Jr., I think you need to get some rest. I can sit with Janet some of the time."

"Im sorry, Jane. I have to be here." His answer was final. He lowered his head back onto the bed. Jane silently left the room.

Every day was like this for the last couple of months. Yet, every day Jane tried to persuade him to take a brake. Jane took over the chores and Hugh Jr. did all of Janet's cares.

Jane new Hugh Jr. needed to get some rest or he would become ill and unable to help his wife. It was no use. He wouldn't leave his wife's side.

Hugh Jr. was sleeping when Jane came into the room to check on Janet. She seemed to be sleeping peacefully. Jane opened the curtain to let in the early morning sun. It looked to be another beautiful spring morning. There was no sign of frost and the lilacs were blooming. Jane opened the window to a sudden aroma that was given off from the purple blooms.

When Jane turned back to attend to Janet, she saw Hugh Jr. was rubbing the sleep from his eyes.

"Good morning, Jane."

"It is a beautiful morning. Just listen to the birds. They are telling us that spring is officially here. Just smell the lilacs. It is almost intoxicating. Oh, I just love this time of the year."

"I do, too. I hope Janet feels up to going outside this afternoon. That's if it is warm enough. Hugh Jr. bent and gave his wife a soft kiss to her forehead. I will go and check the animals while you tend to Janet. I'll see you in about an hour."

This was the first time he left Janet's side other than to eat and toilet. "You go ahead Hugh Jr.; Janet will be okay with me."

He turned and left the room. Jane watched and noticed the slouch in his walk as he went. She could feel the heaviness of his heart.

Jane turned her attention to Janet. Her eyes were open, staring into space. There were black circles around them making them seem even more sunken than they were. The color of them seemed to have faded, as had her body. She was so frail Jane could pick her up and set her in her chair, no longer needing to call for Hugh's help.

Jane put Janet gently into her chair. She was so limp that Jane had to put several pillows around her so as to keep her sitting up. Then Jane changed her bedding and fluffed up her pillows. She put an old cover over the bed and put Janet back on top of the covers so she could clean her up for the day. Janet had become more and more incontinent over the winter. The work load got to be a lot at times. However, Jane didn't mind, for taking care of Janet was what made her desire for life stronger and Jane felt because of this she owed Janet a lot more than she was giving. The last couple of weeks Hugh Jr. had taken over a lot of Janet's care. This took a lot of the burdon from Jane.

After Jane finished getting Janet ready for the day she headed to the kitchen to put on a pot of coffee. Jane didn't get very far when she heard a weak voice.

"Thank you, Jane"

This was the first sign of Janet being awake since Jane had come into the room.

"Janet, good morning, how are you this morning."

"I'm fine."

Janet forced a smile. Just as predicted, she would always put on a happy face. Jane went over to her and sat at her bedside. Lately Janet had been with them so little.

"It is a beautiful day, Janet. The lilacs are in bloom and the birds are singing endlessly. If it is nice later today Hugh Jr. and I will take you out so you can soak up some of the energy around you."

"I would love that, Jane. Where is Hugh Jr. now?"

"He is tending to the livestock. There have been several new calves the last week."

"I would love to see them, Jane."

"Hugh Jr. will take you out there later, Janet. He is so proud of his livestock and loves farming."

"I know. His father was hoping to make a mason out of him, but he loves to farm."

They both jumped as they heard the door open in the next room. It was only Hugh Jr. and they were both laughing when he entered the room.

Jane could see the cloud in his eyes melt when he saw his wife was alert and smiling.

She left the two of them to visit while she made breakfast.

Janet had eaten a few teaspoons of cornmeal mush for breakfast. Then Jane put her down for a nap until lunch and hopped that she would be okay when she woke because Hugh Jr would be upset if Janet wouldn't be able to enjoy that day. At lunch time Jane had to coax her to take a couple of bites of bread, and was glad for what she had eaten, because it was more than she had eaten for days.

After Janet was through eating Jane went to her room for an extra cover and a sweater.

"Do you feel up to going out for a while?"

"I think so, Jane. Will Hugh Jr. be with me?"

"Yes, he will. I think he plans to spend the afternoon pestering you."

"I'd love it."

Jane went out to let Hugh Jr. know that Janet was ready to spend the afternoon out doors with him.

"I'll be right with you. One of the calves managed to get stuck in a small dip in the ground and you would have thought she hadn't seen her mother in a week in stead of a couple of hours." As soon as he had the calf by his mother and eating, he hurried to the house. After washing up he was ready to spend the afternoon with his wife.

While Hugh Jr. was with his wife, Jane decided to go for a ride. After she got the horse and wagon ready she once again rode out to her favorite spot. The sun was beating down upon her back leaving her feeling as though she was wrapped in a warm blanket. The creek beds were running full and the constant rippling added to the peaceful surrounding.

About a mile up the road she saw a doe with her newborn fawn. The mother was trying to get her baby to go into the woods. However, the fawn had a mind of his own. Jane stopped the wagon so as not to startle the mother any more than she was. It was only a matter of minutes when mother and fawn were nowhere to be seen.

Before long, she was guiding the wagon into the churchyard and after tying the horse she headed across the road to her usual spot.

Before she sat down to read, Jane looked around. It seemed she could never get enough of this spot. She noticed the farm below was active. Everything was in miniature form. What few livestock that was there the fall before had multiplied this spring. She could see a man on the other side of the farm house plowing the field from where he had left off the fall before. He was slowly following the plow, stumbling over the turned dirt and his big work horse seemed to go at an even slower pace, dragging the plow, as its blade turned up long even rows of dirt. It didn't seem possible that in the fall there would be tall green stocks of corn in the now black field.

Jane sat back and leaned against the giant old elm. It wasn't long before she felt herself drifting off to sleep. Jane dreamed she was living in the house below. She saw every room in the house and had it decorated to suit her taste. There were two bedrooms with beds that had quilts on them that she had designed and made. The feather pillows were fluffed up with embroidered designs on the covers. The surroundings were crisp and clean. There was a shadow of a man who was watching. Jane turned and was startled when she saw who it was. She let out a slow moan and was jolted back to the present.

Jane felt disappointment and at a loss as she got to her feet and gathered her belongings. She headed back to the wagon knowing it was time to go home and start supper.

The disappointment lingered on the rest of the day. The longing she had for Thomas had never been this strong. At that moment Jane would have given anything to see him. She should never have let what happened get in the way of their love. Jane felt that Thomas must have met someone else and married by now. It had been over two years since she last saw him.

Jane hurried across the road to put her things in the buggy and she made herself busy with the horse until her mind came back to reality. After she got home, she concentrated on fixing super for Hugh Jr. and Janet. They were her life right now and they deserved all she could give.

Janet was alert and vibrant for the next three days. Hugh spent as much time as he could with her. Jane watched them with heartfelt emotion, as they would look into each others eyes and could hear their soft voices as they whispered secrets to each other. Jane tried to stay as far away as she could so as not to disturb them during these intimate times and yet be close enough to be able to go to their aid if need be.

Every time Hugh Jr. called, her heart stopped for a second. Usually it was because he wanted a glass of water for Janet or something simple like that. He and Janet were out under their favorite oak tree. Jane could hear soft laughter coming from their direction.

"Jane, come over here a minute," Hugh Jr. yelled.

Jane hurried to see what it was that he wanted. There in the field was the new colt. It was frolicking around, kicking up his hind legs and twisting from side to side. It was so comical that they all laughed and enjoyed the show, giving him a hearty hand clap in between the different tricks.

Jane thought the colt knew they were watching because he was showing off some unbelievable stunts for a colt that was only a little over a week old. The next thing you know he was finished with his display of talents. The concluding act was him running over to his mother for nourishment.

Janet had been outside for almost two hours. Jane could see she was looking tired. She asked her if she would like to lie down for a while.

Janet responded weakly. "I think I might stay out for another fifteen minutes or so, Jane."

"It's up to you, Janet, but, don't over do it."

"It's such a beautiful day I want to absorb as much of it as I can."

"I don't blame you, Janet. I think I'll to take a ride up to the hill later this afternoon."

"Did you want me to lay down now so you can go, Jane?"

"Oh, no, Janet, there is plenty of day left. You take as much time as you want. I will let you two love birds alone."

"We love birds don't mind you being here, Jane." Both of them chimed in together.

It was almost a half hour before Hugh Jr. brought Janet to her room. Then he went out to make sure everything was okay out in the barnyard, and after taking a toilet break he was ready to spend the afternoon with his wife. When Hugh Jr. entered his wife's room, Jane had just finished making her as comfortable as possible. She looked so pale against the white muslin sheets. She was about to drift off to sleep.

Hugh Jr. thanked Jane and told her to take as much time as she wanted with her ride.

It was a half hour before Jane left. It took her a little longer than usual to hitch up old Nell. Old Nell was feeling a little lazy today. She needed a little coaxing before she would come to her. Jane figured it was because the grass was at its tastiest. Nell didn't really need to eat what she thought she did. She was a huge, old, nag, however, very well mannered and gentle.

Jane enjoyed the sights and sounds around her as she drove out to the hill. It was another beautiful spring day. The birds were loud in the trees and the bees were already pollenating Mother Nature's garden. Janet was still lingering in her thoughts, and Jane said a silent prayer for her.

Janet was napping when Jane got back from her ride. Hugh Jr. was still by her side. His eyes were red and swollen when he turned to Jane.

"She is sleeping so comfortably, Jane. I think I will do the chores early."

"Did you want some help tonight, Hugh Jr.?"

"I need to be alone for a while, Jane. I thought maybe you could stay by Janet in case she awakens"

"Of course, I will be by her side until you get back."

Hugh Jr. was about to close the door behind him. Jane could see he really didn't want to leave.

"Are you sure you don't want me to do the chores tonight, Hugh?"

"It's all right, Jane. I need some time to myself."

His voice was breaking as he spoke.

Jane was alone with Janet. Except for Janets labored breathing, it was so quiet she could hear a pin drop. Janet's breathing was shallow and sporadic. Every once in a while she would stop breathing, making Jane want to shake her. Just as she was about to do just that Janet would suck in a mouthful of air and puff several quick shallow breaths, gradually slowing until she would completely stop breathing again.

When Hugh Jr. finished with the chores he came right back to be by his wife's side. His eyes were even redder and more swollen than when he went out. Jane told him how Janet seemed to stop breathing once in a while and asked him if she should get the doctor.

"I don't think so, Jane. I don't think there is anything the doctor can do. We should let her rest. I think she is fading away and seems not to be in any pain, so let it be as it is meant to be. I will stay with her. You should get as much rest as you can tonight in case I need you to relieve me. I fear it to be a long night."

Jane gave him a big hug before she left. "I'll be right next door if you need me."

She then left Hugh Jr. with his wife and retired to her room for the night. She laid awake for what seemed like hours.

However, Jane must have fallen asleep, because she was awakened from a deep sleep at about two that morning. She could hear Janet breathing in the next room. She seemed to be struggling for each breath she took. Jane grabbed her robe and went to her room. Hugh had a hold of his wife's hand and his head was pressed against it. Jane turned and left the room, although she didn't fall back to sleep.

About an hour later all was quiet in the next room. Jane knew without being told that Janet was no longer with them.

"Jane," Hugh's voice was raspy when he called for her.

Jane entered the room. He still had Janet's hand in his.

"Jane, I want to be with her a little longer. Then I would like you to get her ready for visitors."

"Okay, just call me when you're ready."

Jane went over to him and put her arm around his shoulder. Hugh Jr. began to sob uncontrollably. She then turned to leave him with his grief.

Chapter XXIII

Only the Future

The day of Janet's burial was as beautiful as the day before, when she was out under the oak laughing and visiting with her husband. The undertaker came for the body and Jane and Hugh Jr. followed in their wagon on down the hill to town and back up a steep incline to the small cemetery that was nestled in amongst a stand of enormous pines.

The setting was peaceful and the earth had the smell of spring. The ground was still moist from the melting of the winter snow and the early spring rains. As Jane stepped to the ground her feet sunk a little into the soft pine needles that had built up through the years. There before her was a mound of freshly dug dirt. The hole, where Janet's body was to be placed for the rest of eternity, gapped cold and black.

A horrific and haunted memory flooded Jane's mind as she remembered the foreboding nightmare and felt an icy coldness penetrate her body. She was shivering uncontrollably as she went closer to the menacing black hole. Jane felt she was suffocating as friends and family began to move in closer about her. She was about to turn and run when the minister began to speak. She was able to come to her senses by listening to the words. Although, very little of those words registered in her mind.

The people began to go into the church where there were refreshments. The next thing Jane knew she was alone. She found herself losing control and sobbing, her heart breaking once again. Only this time she vowed to never let her mind go back to the place she had been for so long. She would not hide her pain. She would bear whatever she had to face in life. As these thoughts and feelings were overtaking her, she suddenly was aware of a shadow over her.

Next, there was a hand on her shoulder. She could feel instant warmth permeate her body. Jane unconsciously turned into comforting arms.

She looked up with tears running down her cheeks. Her heart started beating uncontrollably. Jane felt she was in another time, a well-known and comforting place. She gave in to the consoling arms and was unable to pull away for several seconds. Then Jane realized who it was and the situation.

"Thomas, I'm sorry, I didn't know who it was."

"I knew it was you, Jane."

Their eyes were locked. Jane didn't want to blink. She didn't want him to disappear. Next Thomas took a hold of her arm and escorted her into the church. He got some coffee and a sandwich and sat by her while she ate. Jane was unable to speak. She did not know what to say. Thomas sat as silent as she.

After they both had eaten Thomas hesitantly spoke.

"How are you, Jane? I heard you were ill."

"Yes, I was, however, this last year and taking care of Janet has helped me to heal. Seeing how brave Janet was made me realize that you need to get what you can out of life, no matter what the situation might be, because life is short."

"You look tired."

"The last several nights have been restless. I'll have to sleep in tomorrow." Jane shyly smiled at Thomas.

Thomas returned a smile. Jane felt sharp needles in her chest. She sucked in a sudden breath of air. The old feelngs were back. "This can't be possible, thought Jane. It's been so long. How can I still feel this way?" Jane's mind was working way to fast. She felt as though her heart would pound a hole through her chest.

"Jane, are you all right? Do you want me to leave?" Thomas was concerned of how withdrawn Jane had suddenly become.

Jane came back to the present. "I'm okay Thomas. I just don't understand where you came from. You were the last person I expected to see."

"I was in the area, and heard about Janet. Thomas is a good friend of mine you know. My folks have been friends of the family for years. We already knew each other from when we were small and met again in Albany at boarding school. I have been meaning to pay him a visit this last year, but I've been so busy trying to get settled."

"You've been in the area for a year?" Jane could hardly believe what she was hearing.

"Yes I bought some property and have spent almost all my time trying to get settled."

"Is it close to here?" It was hard for Jane to register all she was hearing. She couldn't believe Thomas had been so close. What if she had run in to him? Would she have talked to him or would she have run? The thoughts were consuming her mind.

"Jane, I knew you were staying with Hugh and Janet. I ran into Hugh last week and he said he wouldn't have made it without you."

"You spoke to Hugh last week?"

"Yes I went to Delhi, the first time since I moverd into the area, and he was at the mercantile getting some supplies."

"Hugh didn't say he had seen you."

"I asked him not to say anything to you. I didn't want to upset you when you were needed to help with Janet."

There was another stint of silence. Next, they began to talk about things that didn't include them in the conversation.

Thomas was eager to learn of how Jane's folks were. Jane told him of their plan to sell out. They continued to visit about uneventful things. Thomas didn't reveal anything about his life now or if he was married. They were unaware of anyone else around them unless they were spoken to.

Before they left the church Thomas visited with Hugh for a few minutes, at which time Hugh invited Thomas over for lunch the next day. Jane was full of excitement and found she was acting like a school girl who was in love for the first time.

She didn't get the rest she wanted that night because she couldn't get Thomas from her mind. Jane seemed to remember every aspect of their former relationship and couldn't believe why she thought the way she had before. Now, she most likely, ruined any chance of a life with Thomas.

Jane was up before Hugh. She was busy making cookies and a rhubarb pie when he came into the kitchen.

"Good morning, Jane."

"Good morning. How are you today? Did you get any rest last night?" Jane was still a little nervous about Thomas coming and hoped that Hugh Jr didn't notice.

"I really slept hard, Jane. However, I still feel as though I could sleep another couple of days, non stop."

"I do, too." Jane took a pie from the oven and set it on the table.

"Boy, that sure smells good Jane."

"I hope it tastes as good as it smells."

"I have no doubt that it will."

Jane turned back to the cook stove and got the coffee pot and poured Hugh a cup of coffee.

After Hugh finished with his breakfast he went out to tend to the livestock. Jane was alone with the sadness of lossing a dear friend, and good memories of when she was so in love with Thomas, a love that still burned in her heart.

The morning was gone before Jane knew it. She hurried to her bedroom and changed into something more presentable. She looked in the mirror and found a pale, sad, face. She needed to put some color back. She pinched each cheek with hopes to add a little color. It helped some but knew it would take more than that to bring back the glow she used to have. She hoped Thomas didn't notice.

Jane had just finished brushing her hair back away from her face and pinning it up when she heard Hugh Jr. and Thomas' voices carry into the house from the yard. They both had loud voices and a gift of gab.

Jane was walking into the front room when Hugh Jr. and Thomas came in.

"Hi, Jane," Thomas was beaming as he addressed her.

He looked so handsome in his overhauls and plaid shirt. He wore a straw hat that covered his thick dark hair.

"Hi, Thomas, how are you today?"

"I am great, and you?"

"I'm fine."

Jane put cold roast left over from supper the night before, some fresh biscuits, and cheese, on the table.

After lunch Thomas asked Jane if she would like to go for a ride into the country with him. She was hesitant but decided that she wasn't about to miss the opportunity of spending the day with Thomas. Jane still didn't know if he was married or not but felt if he was he wouldn't ask her to go. She felt as though she was in a dream world when she took Thomas' hand as he helped her into the wagon. Her hand felt that old familiar burn she knew so many years before.

Thomas took a route Jane knew well. They rode in silence most of the way. Then they opened up. First Thomas was telling of what he learned while in college and how he put his skills to work on the farm he had bought.

Jane told Thomas how Janet was instrumental in her recovery and how much she owed her and HughJr.

"Hugh tells me how much he owes you, Jane"

"I think maybe we are even if that's the case."

Before they knew it they were going past the church, Jane's spot on the hill, and on down to the valley below. Jane's heart caught as she viewed the farm she so loved. Once they were at the bottom of the hill Thomas turned the team down a long driveway leading to the farm Jane had watched being built.

"Do you know who owns this place Thomas?"

"Yes, I do, Jane."

"What do you mean?"

"I mean for this to be the farm I built for us, Jane."

Jane was at a loss for words. Thomas stopped beside the big house. She got down from the wagon and looked about her. Her eyes were drawn to the top of the hill and to the spot she came to call her own. She could see the elm tree she had spent so much time reading and dreaming under. It was so small looking at it from this direction. It stood out black against the blue of the sky. It looked so lonely way off from here. Jane turned and faced the farm house and barn noticing how they completed the picture making the scene perfect. Her heart was beating uncontrollably. There were large oak trees scattered here and there around the house. The barn, painted a deep red stood several yards from the house. There was a rail fence across the front of the barnyard.

Jane walked over to the rail fence and leaned against it. Thomas came and stood beside her. They looked off into the horizon; both of them thinking of why it had taken so long for this to happen. They spent the afternoon discussing plans for their future. The day passed quickly and unnoticed by them.

Several times during conversation Jane contemplated telling Thomas what had happened to her. Just as she was about to say something she stopped. Maybe she could someday, but not today. This day was perfect. She had no intention of spoiling her life with Thomas. She hated to keep such a secret from him, but it had been so long ago and she could see no reason to spoil her future again. Maybe someday she would unburden all her demons on Thomas, but that would be another time.

Before they knew it the sun was going down, the hills and the trees were silhouetted black against the sunset; the oranges and yellows blending into pinks and reds. It looked ablaze in the sky, sending rays of hope and peace to come. Jane once again felt calmness in her soul.

ELLEN

Ellen was just a baby when she and her sister were found in an old dry well after an Indian uprising. They were taken in by the person who found her. During her childhood Ellen was happy and carefree. She never remembered the horror of that night. In fact, Ellen had more than most children of that era. She had the luxury of going to England to get an education and the training needed to be a proper young lady, unlike, most children who were born and raised in the wilds of a new country. This book is about Ellen's life after she comes back to America newly married and expecting a child. Only to have her dreams shattered and running not only for her life but also that of her child. She had nowhere to turn and only one person she could trust; the road ahead was dark and sinster.